ROLLIE
& the Rocker

ALSO BY ELIZABETH STEVENS
NEW ADULT/ADULT BOOKS
Heaven & Hell Chronicles
Damned if I do
Damned if I don't
Damned if I know
All Devilbums Go To Heaven

Grace Grayson Security
Chaos & the Geek
Hawk & the Lady
O Lord & the Queen
Rollie & the Rocker
Tank & the Rebel

Loving the Sykes
Caden
Carter
Luther
Oscar
Ashton

MATURE YA/NEW ADULT BOOKS
the Trouble with Hate is…
Accidentally Perfect
Gray's Blade
Being Not Good
Popped

a GRACE GRAYSON novel

ROLLIE
& the Rocker

ELIZABETH STEVENS

KINKY
SIREN

Kinky Siren
An imprint of Sleeping Dragon Books

Rollie & the Rocker
by Elizabeth Stevens

Print ISBN: 978-1925928846
Digital ISBN: 978-1925928839

Cover art by: Izzie Duffield

Copyright 2021 Elizabeth Stevens

Worldwide Electronic & Digital Rights
Worldwide English Language Print Rights

All rights reserved. No part of this book may be reproduced, scanned or distributed in any form, including digital and electronic or mechanical, including photocopying, recording, or by any information storage and retrieval system, without the prior written consent of the Publisher, except for brief quotes for use in reviews. This book is a work of fiction. Characters, names, places and incidents either are the product of the author's imagination or are used fictitiously, and any resemblance to any actual persons, living or dead, events, or locales is entirely coincidental.

*To Arthur,
May you and Ryder have fun over in the
Uncooperative Character Corner.*

♥

Contents

Nora	1
Ryder	17
Nora	40
Ryder	54
Nora	71
Ryder	90
Nora	106
Ryder	126
Nora	137
Ryder	149
Nora	165
Ryder	176
Nora	189
Ryder	198
Nora	207
Ryder	216
Nora	231
Ryder	237
Nora	254
Ryder	263
Grace Grayson Security	285
Tank & the Rebel	286
Rollie & the Rocker	287
Thanks	288
My Books	289
About the Author	290

Author's Note

This book is written using Australian English. This will affect the spelling, grammar and syntax you may be used to. It might come across as typos, awkward sentences, poor grammar, or missed/wrong words. In the majority of cases (I won't claim it's infallible, despite all best efforts), this is intentional and just an Aussie way of speaking (it took my US beta readers a bit to get used to). I can't say 'the' Aussie way, since we seem to differ even within the same state. Just think of us as a weird mix of British and US vernacular and colloquialisms, but with our own randomness thrown in. I still hope you enjoy it, though!

1
Nora

The noise rang in my ears even through my plugs. The reverberation seemed to match the beat of my heart so well it almost felt like it was powering every heartbeat, that I would crumble to nothing and cease existing when silence descended.

Relief flooded me.

I'd made it.

One more down.

I'd reached the checkpoint safely and it wasn't

quite time to worry about the next one yet. Let me bask in the glow of this one for just a little bit longer before the weight of the world and reality set in.

I looked to Brax, who was already strutting toward the front of the stage with his arms in the air and whipping the screaming crowd into even more of a frenzy. Zach was jumping around, in full showman mode. Nate was threatening to kick over his drumkit in excitement. And Cooper was looking at me. I shrugged at him, trying to get him off my case.

Last thing I needed was my older brother being all overprotective and oppressive.

When I'd begged Cooper to let me try out for his band, I'd never imagined that we'd be playing to worldwide crowds. All I'd wanted was to spend some time with my brother and bond over the love of music I'd cultivated especially for that purpose. Irrelevant were thoughts of future fame and fortune. Irrelevant were his three hot friends who hung out in our garage on a near daily basis like they didn't have their own homes to haunt. I just wanted a place where I finally felt I belonged.

While I had found that – I'd ended up with three extra brothers I didn't want and couldn't live without – I'd also fallen down a rabbit hole of expectations and found an inordinate inner fear of letting people down.

So, I'd agreed when the boys wanted to start getting an audience on YouTube. I agreed when they wanted to do gigs around Adelaide. I agreed when they wanted to try gigs interstate. I agreed when they wanted to move to the States and make a 'proper' go of it. I agreed when the boys wanted to sign the contract.

I wasn't against any of it necessarily, I just had some reservations, some more options I would have explored, some more time I would have taken to think it all through. But, in the face of their excitement, I couldn't bear the thought of disappointing them. So, we five of us ran in full tilt and never looked back.

It was a sensible idea, not looking back.

Had I looked back, I would have seen more clearly how the stage persona that had once started out as a joke had completely overtaken who I was. I might have had time to miss who I was and maybe realised that standing on a stage in front of thousands of people was actually quite daunting.

But I didn't do any of that.

I stayed firmly in the moment. The furthest I

looked was our next concert.

We did a couple of encores and headed off the stage. As soon as I was out of sight of the crowd, arms were around me and ushering us towards the green room. I kept my eyes peeled for my chance.

It wasn't until we were in the green room that they all finally took their eyes off me, thinking that someone else was still making sure I didn't wander. But the one guy who'd been hired for that job, Gavin, had been distracted by our manager, Emma, who thought that Coop would have eagle eyes on me the way he usually did.

But Coop was trying to settle the latest argument between Nate and Brax.

I grabbed my go bag and slipped out of the room. I pulled my sunglasses on and covered my distinctive bright red hair in a dark baseball cap before I slid into the darkness of the cleaning cupboard, knowing it would only be a minute at most before someone missed me.

"Nora?" I heard Zach call, obviously the first one to realise I was gone.

"Miss Fern!" I heard Gavin call to Emma. "Did you see her?"

"No," Emma called back, their voices getting more distant. "Damn her. She's gone."

She wasn't, but she soon would be, I thought to myself as I checked the coast was clear before slipping out through the back fire exit I knew for a fact wasn't armed.

There was a small, poorly lit alley behind the venue. Only once I was in it did I breathe a truly easy breath. Only there did I feel released of all the pressures of the band, the tour, the fans, myself. I felt light and free and not like I was just living for the next concert.

I took a step out of the darkness of the door and looked up to the light. For a moment, all the endorphins rushed back as I stared into the light streaming onto my face. I pulled my sunglasses off and put them in my pocket.

As I took a step towards the main road at the other end of the alley, there was a clatter. I looked down, but I hadn't kicked anything.

Something – or someone – else was in the alley with me.

My heart beat harder as I hoped it was just some animal knocking about for scraps of food in the bins. There was nothing else. No movement. No noise.

I took another step and there was another clatter. Like maybe someone was stepping at the same time as me.

Then, a voice was coming out of the shadows between me and the main road. It was singing. Singing a truly bastardised version of one of our songs. The only track I sang lead on. Whoever was singing it, had slowed it right down. Like more than even the acoustic version Nate had convinced me to do. And their breathing. It rasped. That was the closest I could come to describing it. It was too breathy, off-pitch.

The sound alone was enough to send goosebumps crawling across my skin, but being unable to see the singer made my heart thud. A chilled shiver ran from my heart and down to my fingers, into my legs, keeping me firmly rooted to the spot.

My heart raced so fast, it was hard to keep my breath.

What had seemed like an escape now felt like a cage. The fire exit had locked to this side when I closed it behind me. The only way I was getting out of there was past the shadow and into the main road.

But that would require me going past the disembodied singer.

I was sure whoever was singing it accidentally changed it to minor key. Not quite – the whole thing was totally off any key I recognised – but the same vibe. It better suited some Kubrick horror film.

"Nora!" I heard Gavin call from the direction of the fire exit I hadn't heard open.

I looked towards his voice, then back into the shadows. But the singing had stopped.

"Nora!" Gavin said again, holding the door open while reaching out to me.

I shuffled backwards into his arms, my eyes

unable to leave the shadows as he pulled me back inside.

"Was that him?" I asked Gavin as the fire exit closed again.

I finally looked away and up at him. The guy was big. Tall and wide. You just knew his muscles had muscles. He had security written all over him. And that was even without the crisp suit he insisted on wearing. He looked liked he'd fit right in guarding the president of the US with his little earpiece and everything.

And I really would think of anything to avoid my issues, wouldn't I?

Gavin looked towards the door and shook his head. "Maybe, Miss Curry."

And we were back to the 'Miss Curry' nonsense.

"Nora!" came Emma's voice from further up the

hall. "Gavin, you found her."

"Outside."

Emma stopped in front of me. "You're white as a sheet."

I huffed a laugh. "I'm fine."

Emma looked at Gavin. "What happened?"

I shrugged and answered for Gavin. "Nothing. Fan. They were singing."

"Fan?" Emma asked Gavin.

Gavin shrugged. "Maybe."

Emma's eyes narrowed and she turned on her heel and marched back to the green room. "Nora!" she snapped.

I hurried after her and Gavin managed to keep up perfectly well with his long stride.

"That is it! We're suspending the tour," Emma yelled when I'd caught up, throwing her hands in the air in exasperation.

It was rare that our manager raised her voice at us and even more rare that it was directed at me. To the point that it had never been directed at me.

The others were still in the green room, winding down with a drink and a few pizzas.

"What?" I cried, looking around at them.

"Tell them," Emma said, waving a hand at me. "Tell them what just happened."

I shrugged again. "Nothing. There was someone outside the fire exit. They…sang one of our songs when I came out."

"Which one?" Nate asked, leaning forward in his chair.

My shrug was about as nonchalant as I could make it. "*Firebird*."

"What?" Zach asked.

Emma nodded. "Yeah. You know who that was?"

"We don't know that," I said quickly, pushing away the remnants of the feeling I'd had in the alley.

"We can't risk it," Nate said.

"He's never come to a concert before," Zach said.

"That we know of."

"And he might never come again. There's no reason to suspend the tour," I told them all. "It's stupid."

"This is your safety we're talking about, Nora," Brax said harshly. "It's not a fucking joke."

"I'm not the first person who's ever had a stalker and I won't be the last. Nothing needs to be suspended. People are counting on us."

Which was what I lived for. I had to live for it. If I didn't live for it, then I had nothing to live for.

"I don't care. They'll care more if you never make

more music than missing a couple of concerts."

"Yeah, and when nothing comes of it, they'll be super pissed off that we missed concerts for nothing."

"Nothing comes of it? NOTHING?" Cooper shouted from the corner of the room.

He stood up and skulked over to us.

"You've just gone and ditched your fucking security *again*," he pointed at Gavin, "and this stalker fucker has got way too close for comfort. When will you take this seriously? The shit this dude is saying…" Cooper didn't beg for much, but he was begging me to listen now. "Nora, if he gets close to you…"

I sighed. "So, your answer is to bench me?"

"What else can we do if you're going to keep making a joke of this?" Emma asked.

"And that's your final answer?" I asked.

Gavin and Emma exchanged a look. Something silent seemed to pass between them.

"We might have one more option…" Emma said slowly.

"Great." I nodded. "Let's do that."

Emma looked at me sternly. "We'll see what we can do. In the meantime, when we get back to Adelaide, you need to stay at the hotel and not leave unless you're at the venue."

Oh, no. My worst nightmare. Stuck at the hotel. With nothing else to do but wear my comfiest trackies, down tub after tub of Rainbow Paddle Pop ice cream, and binge my favourite trashy movies. What a pity.

But I couldn't say any of that.

"Fine," I huffed like I was put out about the whole

thing. "Fine. Whatever. Home or venue. Fine."

2
Ryder

The world had stilled to slow motion. Noise was muffled, existing outside the ringing in my ears. My pulse thumped in my temples. The stench of blood filled my nose. My body burned from exertion.

I could hear the gunfire in the base of my skull. I could feel the near-misses whizzing by my face. My adrenalin was through the roof. I could feel my heart pounding in my chest. O Lord's voice was muffled in my ear. I was too busy worrying about that blood soaking through Tank's fatigues as he lay on the ground. Hawk was shouting something, but his voice sounded further away than O Lord's. Chaos was shaking me, then his hand smacked me across the face–

Only it wasn't his hand. It was Folger's. And it had been just what I needed to pull me out of the memory. Folger's left hook never failed to get the job done in the ring.

The ring.

The closest I could come to sorting my shit.

The closest I came to letting the memories in without getting lost in them.

The ring let me release my anger, my frustration and my fear. But it also let me wallow in it. It reminded me of all the pain we went through. It went some way to giving me the punishment I felt I deserved for everything I'd done, good cause or not.

I grinned at Folger. "You got lucky."

"Yeah?" he sneered. "You wanna see me get lucky again?"

"I have a strict play not watch policy and I'm afraid I don't share."

"What?" Folger's hands dropped just enough.

I threw my right fist forward. It smashed into his nose with a satisfying thud and jolt of pain to my knuckle, even through my wrapping. Folger's head cracked back and he was on the floor.

McKay did the count and called the knock out.

I ducked out of the ring as a couple of others rushed in to clear Folger out before the next match.

"You want in again?" Mickey asked, counting his winnings.

My heart hammered and I breathed heavily. I

could feel the thud of my pulse in my eye socket. Madness dictated I say yes. That madness that was oh so tempting. Half the fun was living on the edge of temptation. I shook my head.

"Nah, can't send all your best blokes to the ER," I joked.

Mickey gave me a smirk. "So long as my best keeps in fighting form," he said, indicating me with a nod.

I wiped my nose before I started unwrapping my hands. "You know I make no promises."

"Ah," he scoffed. "You'll be back. You always are."

I wasn't going to dignify that with a response, so I just gave him a nod and headed for the locker room.

By the time I was showered and changed, Folger was wandering in.

"That Tank of yours taking new clients?" he joked.

I smirked. "Nah. He's on a job."

Folger nodded. "You let me know when he's back and I might consider signing up."

"You think he'll teach you how to beat me?" I asked with a knowing smile.

Folger nodded again. "I reckon so. Definite when I tell him it's to beat you."

I snorted. "Yeah. Probably."

"See you next week?"

I shrugged. "Dunno. We'll see what the calendar has in store."

"You and yer fancy wankers."

I nodded and gave him another smile as I headed out. "Me and my fancy wankers."

"That's one of the better shiners I've seen on ya,

mate," O'Neil said as I walked out of the locker room.

I nodded. "Must have been a bit slow today."

"Might be time to tell that boss of yours what you get up to on a Friday night, eh?"

"We'll see. 'Night, man."

"See ya later, Ryder."

With my luck, I wouldn't have to tell Chaos shit.

I tended to heal fast. Always had. A fight on Friday night with my skills saw me work-ready on Monday. Not unblemished, but healed enough for 'hard training with Tank' to be a legitimate excuse for the clientele. I was lucki*er* that my bosses ignored bumps, bruises, cuts or scrapes unless they were actively bleeding on anything they shouldn't; things we got up to, they could have come from anywhere.

Besides, I wasn't the one they usually sent on the fancy gigs. Didn't mean I saw none of the action, but my jobs were normally the sort that a few bruises just cemented the right image. Mr Nelson always worried and insisted I have a cup of tea before we got into work. But Jefferson in particular quite liked how it made me, in his words, extra intimidating. Which went a long way to explain what kind of business he liked to think he ran. Still wasn't as bad as Falkner, though.

And the Grace Grayson boys were nothing if not excellent at playing a part.

****

The next Thursday, I was hanging out with Flo under the guise of organising my calendar. Because I was that good at organisation.

"So, Mrs Fortescue has a lunch tomorrow–" Flo started.

"Is that the one I need the tux for?" I asked, making sure my tie wasn't in danger of being too tight.

Flo looked up at me, her face a beacon of exasperated fondness hiding behind a wry smirk. "That's Mr Nelson on Saturday. Honestly, how do you get such good reviews?"

I shrugged. "I live in the moment." I waved my hand at her. "All this planning and looking to the future bullshit *detracts from the now, darling.*"

Flo snorted. "Sure, Edna."

"That's on Hank. He's made me watch that about a thousand times."

"You've babysat twice."

"He's got me watching it in my dreams, Flo."

Flo laughed. "He loves it. He wants to be Dash when he's older."

"I can see Archie being more like Violet."

Flo nodded. "Sounds about right. Now, you've distracted me. Mrs Fortescue–"

We were unfortunately interrupted by the ding of the elevator. Flo and I both turned to see who was coming out. And, blow me down, it was a sight for sore eyes.

"Honey," I called to the offices at large. "Tank's home!" I looked him over. "But, seriously, aren't you meant to be on tour?"

Tank sighed. "We're all supposed to be on tour."

I pulled up the calendar on my phone and saw the band was scheduled to play at home that weekend. "Ah, pit stop. Nice you found time for your old friends."

His smile was weary. "Good to see you, too." He nodded to Flo. "Flo."

"Hey, Tank," she said with a smile.

"Tank? Rollie?" our liege called from his office. "A word?"

I looked to Tank. "I can think of a million reasons why *I'm* being called to the principal's office, but what did you do?"

"He'll explain."

I patted the top of Flo's desk and followed Tank to Chaos' office and plonked myself down in one of the chairs. "'Sup, bossman?"

Chaos spared me the smallest look of exasperation before Tank sat down and the boss launched into it.

"Tank's…got a challenge on his hands," Chaos

started.

"Understatement," the big guy mumbled.

Chaos gave him a sympathetic look. "We've all been there."

"So, this doesn't have anything to do with the computer backgrounds in Nico's office…?" I asked slowly.

"What computer backgrounds in Nico's office?" Chaos asked, his face going from direct business-minded to confusedly caught-out.

I was slightly relieved. "Ah. Good. So, if not that, why am I–?"

"ROLLIE!!" the resident nerd screamed from his office. "I am going to *kill* you. Strangle you. See how you like dismemberment! I'll dust off my stash of explosives and tie them all to you before I set each one off individually. I don't care that's not how it works. I'm doing it. I'm going to– Oh, hey, Tank." Nico's rant stopped dead as he pulled up in Chaos' door.

Tank nodded. "Same old?"

Nico frowned at me. "Worse."

I shrugged. "I thought I'd zhuzh up the place."

"What Raegan and I do or don't do is no business of yours!"

Chaos sighed. "What did you do?" he asked me.

"Who doesn't like fluffy bunnies and girls in wedding dresses?" I countered.

Nico huffed. "His Photoshop skills are abysmal, by the way."

"I did that on my phone!" I told him indignantly. "What do you expect?"

Based on Nico's sneer, I'd hit the sweet spot. He was sufficiently annoyed to yell and gripe and curse me out, but not annoyed enough to do anything but destroy all my hard work and then get on with his life. My person was safe from retaliation.

It was more than I deserved, but less than I expected.

Nico cocked his head to the side. "His desktop display skills, on the other hand. Better than I'd have expected." There was a note of pride in his voice.

"I practised," I said with a smile.

All pride was gone. "You keep Raegan out of your shenanigans." His tone was warning enough, but he added a jutting finger as well.

"What?" I asked the expectant faces of Tank and Chaos. "We've had one wedding, surely we're due another one?" I looked at Chaos pointedly.

Chaos kicked his chin to me, giving me an equally pointed look. "Yeah? Why don't you find a girl and it can be yours?"

I huffed at him and slouched in my chair. "'Cos it's as easy as that," I grumped.

The annoyed, exasperated and slightly amused faces all turned to sympathy and that was worse.

Two years ago, I hadn't had this problem. It had been me and my mates and my casual hookups – not at the same time, obviously – and life had been good. Well, as good as could be with the post-special ops PTSD. But the team at Grace Grayson had lived it all together. We knew each other's demons inside out.

Problem was, the others weren't just hardwired to deal with those demons better, they were also finding people to help them bear it in ways we couldn't help each other no matter how much we cared.

Chaos, team leader and now CEO, was fully loved up with his best friend's little sister. The guy, who was darker than the rest of us combined, now strode our fair halls humming. His past wasn't forgotten, but it was overshadowed by his future.

Hawk, second only to our leader, was the first of us married and sickeningly happy about it despite the short lead up. His relationships with his sister and Chaos had been what got him through everything, including his two favourite people getting together behind his back.

Nico was as grouchy as ever, but any idiot could see how hard he'd fallen for his nerd queen. He'd always been a cynic and withdrawn, long before any of our missions affected us. Which wasn't to say he was unaffected, but he'd changed the least of us.

Tank of the perpetual single just had coping mechanisms down. Always had. He had one of those strong constitutions that saw him deal with his problems in a healthy way, unlike the rest of us. How he was friends with the rest of us and put up with our damaged arses, I'd never know.

Which left me being me. I wouldn't call myself delicate, but I'd always favoured avoidance instead of dealing with my shit. Letting it all build up in the background to nice unhealthy levels of damaged psyche. But I wasn't going to bring the rest of them down with my lack of ability to cope, so the humour that had once masked a lack of self-confidence was now a humour that masked deep inner pain. I'd made myself the joker so we could all feel lighter.

It was great for self-preservation and to distract me from my darker thoughts, but was fucking useless for forming real attachments to people who didn't know me as well as the Grace Grayson boys did. Particularly people of the female variety. Colour me not surprised that, when they were looking for more than a one-night stand, they were looking for someone who didn't make a joke out of everything from lost lippie to dead pets. I considered myself lucky I never got far enough for them to notice I lacked depth or that I had a wall up that gave China a run for its money.

It was a blessing and a curse.

I was too much of a mess to be any good for a cat, let alone a girlfriend. But that didn't stop a part of me wanting it. It didn't stop a part of me knowing I was ready. That I did want it. Wanted what my friends were finding. Because, at the rate they were going, Tank was going to pull a fiancée out of the proverbial woodwork and I was going to be the stunted ninth wheel whose jokes got more desperate as the years of solitude piled on to the point they stopped inviting me anywhere.

I so didn't want to be that guy.

"Besides," I chirped to the room to lift the mood, "what kind of girl would tie my free spirit down?"

Chaos looked at some papers on his desk. "I have a feeling I know."

I sat forward with interest. "Oh, yeah?"

Nico gave a snort that he wasn't about to let be a laugh. "Look at him. Mad keen."

"Why don't you shut up and go sort out your desktops?" I shot back.

Nico looked at me with death glares. "Like I need *more* work to do. Thanks," he huffed sarcastically before turning on his heel and walking out."

"As I was saying," Chaos said before I could make a well-timed quip about Nico. "Tank's got a hard case." He pointed at me. "Don't." I smirked and

Chaos fought a return smile. "Nora Curry."

The name sounded vaguely familiar, but I couldn't place why. "What about her? Who is she?" If they told me she was Tank's new squeeze, I was going to lose it. Now didn't seem like a new squeeze announcement, though.

"The bassist for *Valjean*," Tank said roughly. I could tell just what he thought about her from those four words.

I looked between them and felt my mouth drop open. "No…" I breathed. "Tank's VIP is One-Night Nora?!"

We'd all had Tank's schedule, but I'd been way too lazy to Google who was playing on those dates and no one else had cared enough.

But One-Night Nora of *Valjean* fame?

I felt like a little boy at Christmas who knows that

the BMX he'd been desperately wishing for all year was waiting for him under the tree. Not that I'd ever found the long-awaited BMX under any tree.

Chaos nodded.

I snorted. I tried not to. I failed. "No wonder he's having problems."

"Miss Curry is very…strong-willed," Tank muttered.

It wasn't like Tank to have a cross word to say about anybody. Unless that body was me or Hawk and then we probably – definitely – deserved it.

"Miss Curry wasn't terribly pleased that her manager hired security for her, let alone that the security who turned up was…" Chaos petered off, unwilling to even accidentally insult the gentle giant before him.

I had no such qualms. "The great big fun police?"

Tank glared at me but said nothing.

Chaos looked like he was about to say something that he really didn't want to say. "We've been talking with *Valjean*'s manager, Miss Fern, and come to the conclusion that what Miss Curry needs is someone who can keep her under control by letting her be out of control."

Oh, fuck the BMX. *This* was sounding like all my dreams come true.

I looked between them, not quite willing to believe what I thought they were saying. "So…let me get this straight. You're firing Tank–"

"Reassigning is a better word," Chaos interjected.

"*Firing* Tank," I repeated with glee. "And you want me to take over. With a VIP?"

A wicked bubbly giggle was threatening in my chest. Hell had to have frozen over if Mr Steady And

Reliable was being subbed out for little old me. And, fuck yeah, I did have a great opinion of myself.

Chaos and Tank looked at each other and Chaos nodded resignedly.

"Yes," he finally said. "I'm firing Tank from a VIP job and replacing him with you."

I tipped my hand at him coquettishly. "Oh, shucks. You do know how to flatter a boy."

Chaos smiled. "Yes, I do."

"When do I start?" I asked, looking between them.

"Today," Tank said.

Something else dawned on me. "I'm going on tour with *Valjean*…"

Chaos nodded. "You're going on tour with *Valjean*."

I knew what his next words would be. I nodded

subconsciously at him. "Yeah. Yeah. Face of the company. Behave and all that."

I'd work out the details in due course. The important thing was, I was going on tour with a world-famous rock band!

3
Nora

"Why don't we just lower him into position?" Nate said as he twirled his drumsticks in his fingers. "He'll be starkers 'cept for a pair of black wings and his guitar covering his bits."

Brax frowned at his twin. "Bit melodramatic, don't you think?"

Nate nodded. "I do think. But we're talking about you, not me."

"In that case," Brax drawled. "Why don't we get

you ridin' in on a chariot pulled by flaming peacocks?"

"Interesting imagery. Don't think the animal cruelty thing is us. Thoughts?" Nate asked as he looked around at us.

Coop looked like he was composing some new concerto on an invisible piano.

Zach was reading a book.

That left me stupidly being the only one paying even the vaguest amount of attention to the squabbling twins.

"Nora?" Nate pressed.

"He can be naked, too," Brax said, like that was a bonus.

When it came to the Glenn twins and a disagreement, they lost all signs of machismo and charm and turned into two little boys fighting on the playground about who could pee the furthest. If only the tabloids could see them now, they'd have a field day. But we all had baggage we wanted to keep private. Some of us more than others.

I shrugged. "I don't care which of you is naked. It's all the same to me."

Which was, as intended, the worst thing to say to them.

"Just because we're identical," started Brax.

"Doesn't mean we're the same person," finished Nate before he turned to Brax. "You know, I reckon we should use some of that footage from…"

And he and Brax went to work on revamping our backing video.

My barb had done its job. It had turned their attention away from each other and united them against me. The only way the band functioned was if the Glenn twins were united against something, rather than against each other. They were the powerhouse behind what made *Valjean* well…*Valjean*.

More often than not, I took the fall and let that something be me. I was used to putting anything and everything in front of my ego, my self-esteem, my self-worth. It had become my brand. It was who I was. Sometimes, I missed the Nora that floated around my memory in fragments. More often, I didn't have the time or luxury to be anything other than what sold our music.

"Nora," Emma said as she poked her head into the room.

Nate made the kind of 'oo' noise that made it sound like I was being called to the principal's office.

I threw him a poked tongue before turning to Emma. "Yeah?"

She gave me an apologetic grimace. "Need to have a chat with you about…" She lowered her voice to a stage whisper like that was going to make it better, "your security."

I made a good show of huffing and puffing about the unfairness of it all as I hauled myself out of my chair and followed our manager out to the corridor.

Gavin was with her. And so was a guy I recognised from a picture I'd seen on Gavin's computer once by chance. He was another member of the Grace Grayson security team.

He was shorter than Gavin, by a long shot – but, then everyone was – with reddish-brown hair. He was well-built, not too skinny and not too muscular, and carried himself with the self-confidence of a man who knew who he was and what he was doing with his life. Had I been a suit-loving chick, I'd have swooned over the way he filled out the perfectly tailored fabric clinging to his body. He had a cheeky look to him. The kind of cheek I'd like. You could see it in the way his green eyes sparkled as he took me in as closely as I was taking him in.

"Nora, this is Ryder Andrews. He works with Gavin at Grace Grayson," Emma told me.

"It bring your mate to work day?" I asked.

Ryder smirked and I felt an unnecessary ping of pride in my chest. This total stranger had done more to validate me than Gavin had in months of hanging out with him. I somehow knew Ryder got it. He got the sass. He got the joke. He knew where it came from and what it meant. I couldn't help smiling back at him.

"Ryder's here for hand over," Gavin said in his deep and rumbly voice.

I looked at him in confusion. I looked at Emma for explanation. I looked at Ryder mostly because I liked looking at him, but also like it'd help me understand Gavin's words.

"What do you mean? Hand over? Me? You're handing me over?" I asked, looking between Gavin and Ryder. "You're quitting?" I accused Gavin.

I may not have been thrilled when Emma hired Gavin as extra security for me. I may have given him the slip anytime I could. I may have even been less friendly with him than I could have been. But I was feeling more amenable to this whole added security thing after the other night, and Gavin was a straight up decent guy. I didn't want to have to get to know someone new. Not even someone clearly as sinfully gorgeous and delightfully mischievous as this Ryder Andrews.

"We thought perhaps you and Gavin weren't a…great fit," Emma said.

"Great fit?" I huffed sarcastically. "Great fit? Who's ever a great fit with their security detail?"

"Fine," Emma said. "Putting it plainly, Nora. You've been a brat and Grace Grayson are reassigning your security to someone more likely to keep you in line."

I noticed Gavin and Ryder exchange a look and wondered what exactly they'd said about me. Gavin had been no stranger to towing the hard line. He hadn't been shy about putting his foot down. What was Ryder like for them to think he'd be more likely to keep me in line. The look in his eyes told me he wasn't the ruthlessly strict type. But I knew as well as anyone that looks could be deceiving.

"Miss Fern. Miss Curry," Ryder started. "Tank–Gavin has an exemplary record. His service record's even better. But Grace Grayson works because we all have different skill sets. My skills, we feel, are…more suitable to the situation."

"Mr Grace assured me–" Emma started, looking somewhat annoyed. I just didn't know if it was with Mr Grace or me.

Ryder nodded. "Our availability changes–"

"Oh, no," Emma said, throwing me a pointed look. "I'm not blaming anyone at Grace Grayson. Even I failed to see how difficult Nora would be."

I frowned at her and crossed my arms over my chest like a petulant child.

"Jobs change," Ryder said, doing all the talking for Gavin, just as he liked it. "If that means we need to shift our schedules around, we do. We want to be as…accommodating to our client's needs as possible."

I did not imagine the way he looked at me then. I know I didn't. His eyes clearly said that he was willing to cater to any and every need I might have, no matter how personal. I was heavily considering taking him up on it.

Gavin actually used his words here. "We've talked it over and feel that Ryder will be able to do the job to Miss Curry's satisfaction."

I felt like they'd practiced their lines the whole way here.

I also felt like Ryder would be able to do a great many things to my satisfaction.

Most notably, I was annoyed that Gavin was ditching me.

"I didn't think Gavin was the kind to give up," I said.

"I think that says more about you than it does about him," Emma replied ruefully.

"Oi," I argued. "I take exception to that."

"You can do whatever you like," Emma said. Then muttered, "You usually do."

My arms dropped as I was feeling less like the petulant child and more like the one who knew they'd done wrong and wanted to put things right. I hadn't just annoyed Emma. I'd disappointed her. Until the chance came and I reverted to my usual self again, I'd be repentant.

Gavin looked at me with a sigh. "At Grace Grayson, we pride ourselves on getting a job done. We do what we need to do, depending on the clients' needs. If that means stepping away, then that's what we have to do."

I was pretty sure it was the longest continuous thing that had ever come out of his mouth.

"What Gavin means," Ryder added, "is that we put our clients first and our egos second. And trust me, Gavin's got the smallest ego of the lot of us."

Why did it sound like he didn't mean 'ego' when he said it?

I gave him a knowing smirk and he returned it tenfold.

"We've got a new plan for your security, Miss Curry," Ryder went on, his eyes scanning my body like that was of utmost importance. "And we feel I'm better suited to the new plan."

I was intrigued to hear about this new plan.

"And if we do the new plan, I don't have to be benched anymore?" I asked.

Emma nodded. "You follow the new plan and the tour will continue as advertised. None the wiser."

"Okay." I smiled at them all. "I can get behind that."

"And I'll be behind you," Ryder said.

I was sure I saw Gavin give him a look that was at once fond exasperation and warning. Ryder just grinned, first at Gavin, then at me and winked.

Oh, I liked Ryder. I really liked Ryder. I wanted-to-take-him-straight-to-my-bedroom liked Ryder. That godforsaken twinkle in his eye that was begging to get me into all kinds of trouble was also doing a really weird thing to me. It made me hesitate. It made me hold my tongue. It made me want to…get to know him.

"Lord help us," Emma muttered with a smile.

I seconded that.

I was going to need all the help I could get when it came to avoiding Ryder's obvious charm.

4
Ryder

Nora-freaking-Curry was standing in front of me.

Better yet, Nora-freaking-Curry was clearly checking me out.

Even better, she knew I was checking her out and she seemed to like it.

She looked nothing and everything like the pictures.

Fire-engine red hair. Big, sultry chocolate eyes. Hips you could hold onto wrapped in tight ripped black jeans. She had curves in all the right places, showing clearly even under the generic Rolling Stones' mouth tank. She wore monster black heels that put her taller than me. She exuded rock goddess and, still, she was more casual than she was in shoots or on stage.

I was envisioning what it would be like to have those long legs wrapped around me, but I knew better than to push my luck too quickly and blow my…chances.

Tank's tight little panties were already worked into a knot over the very little I'd let slip. I hated to think what he'd be like if he knew the intimate details going on in my head – because, let's be honest, he knew enough vagaries just to make him blush. I was strong, but not nearly strong enough to catch him if he fainted.

Nora wasn't the first client I'd been attracted to. I doubted she'd be the last. The fellas from Grace Grayson hadn't given themselves a fantastic reputation among the high society ladies for our all-star service because we saw a lot of action…on the streets. Now, in the sheets? Well, that was the worst best rumour we had. Whether one believed it or not tended to depend on what one thought about one's wife.

Whether I saw any action of the more personal kind with Nora Curry, time would tell. But there was a spark. There was potential. There were the flutterings of eyelids, the coquettish smiles, and the evaluating glances of the interested. And, she was giving me the same signs in return.

Tank was giving me his own signs, but I was much less interested in being told to keep it in my pants.

"If that's everything, I'll leave you to it," Tank said, but there was warning in his voice and eyes; behave, get the job done, you're the face of the company here.

I nodded to him and his eyebrow rose for a moment. I nodded again as I rolled my eyes, and finally he eased up on me.

"I guess this is goodbye, then, Gavin," Nora said, rocking on her feet.

Tank nodded to her. "You're in good hands."

Nora gave him a smile. "I don't doubt that."

Nora thrust her hand out and Tank shook it.

"Do my eyes deceive me or is that a tear in the big fella's eye?" I teased.

Tank merely looked at me with a raised eyebrow.

"Aw, shucks," I told him as I batted his arm

playfully. "You always know just what to say."

Nora snorted what sounded like a very involuntary snort, then coughed like she was covering it up.

Miss Fern looked at Tank as if she was asking if there were actually two of them and Tank seemed to answer 'yes'. I grinned and looked at Nora. She grinned back.

If my job was to keep her under control by letting her lose control, it looked like we were heading for success. I saw the same lightbulb on in Tank's eyes.

He gave me one more loaded look, gave us all a nod, and headed off.

"So, what do you need first?" Miss Fern asked me.

I shouldn't have looked at Nora – there was professionalism and there was professionalism – but

I did. Once done, all I could do was go with it. I had my fill of drinking in that unique gorgeousness, and turned back to her manager.

"I guess I should chat to your usual security, get the lay of the land," I said. "Gav said this was sound check and show's tonight?"

Miss Fern nodded. "I'll take you to them. What do you want to do with Nora?"

Oh, she had to stop giving me those lines. Nora and I exchanged another heated look, but my mind was heading into spec and recon territory and that meant flirting was taking a back seat.

"I trust you won't be sneaking off in the next half hour?" I asked her, using my big boy, superior tone.

She had the decency to hide her amusement. "I'll...*behave*."

Oh, damn. Oh, damn. Oh, damn. Oh. *Damn*.

Would this woman be the death of me? Would that even be so bad? Death by her was way better than any of the near-misses we'd had on missions. Definitely had at least one up on kidnapping and torture.

I couldn't help but wink. "Good girl."

I let Miss Fern lead me away to find the security guys.

"I'm trusting your process…" she started slowly and I knew where her mind was going.

"I could say a lot of things that might put your mind at ease, Miss Fern," I told her. "But the crux of it is that, despite outward appearances, I do know what I'm doing. She's safe with me."

The manager nodded, but I could see she was still worried.

"You care about her," I said, trying to lower my

voice into that gentle tone Chaos was way better at than me.

Miss Fern sighed. "She's just not taking the threats seriously. And then the other night... I don't think she'll ever admit just how much it affected her. She was so scared, but there was that brave face. She wouldn't admit it, but she was...a bit dusty on the flight home."

I nodded. I could only imagine. When I'd heard about it, I'd felt a chill. The violation of knowing someone was watching you from the shadows wasn't foreign to me. I'd been on both sides of the coin and neither had been pleasant. The truly chilling thing was that it was probably pleasant for whoever this arsehole was. I didn't blame Nora for getting pissed after.

"We've got five more stops on the tour?" I

checked and she nodded. "Okay. And what are the plans for after?"

Miss Fern looked at me, shock on her face. "What do you mean?"

"Well, is this a tour-only kind of deal? What about when the tour's over and Miss Curry's at home alone?"

Miss Fern swore under her breath. "I never even… We've all been so focussed on the tour…"

I nodded. "Don't worry. We'll take each step as it comes up. Maybe it'll never come up."

"If it was him the other night, it's the first time he's done anything offline."

"Great. That's a good sign. Hopefully, it was just coincidence. He lived there and took the opportunity. The number of times this leads to following the band around is minor compared to what goes on the internet under the relative safety of anonymity."

Miss Fern released a deep breath. "Of course. I'm sure you're right. I just… It would be easier if it were…Zach or Nate. They'd do what they were told, when they were told. I wouldn't have to worry they were constantly trying to slip away and be in god knows what danger."

"That's the tough bit," I agreed. "The uncertainty. But, that's why I'm here."

Miss Fern sized me up none too subtly. "Well, she's certainly taken to you much more than she took to Gavin."

"I tend to have that effect on people," I told her.

She smiled a knowing smile. "I'll leave it up to you to decide on the sense of accepting her invitation."

"Invitation?"

"To her bed, Ryder," she said wryly. "Her invitation to her bed."

I hadn't been playing dumb. I'd legitimately not expected her manager to be so on top of her affairs. Here I was, thinking maybe I was going to be invited to one of those music awards nights.

"Ah." I gave a nod. "Right. Well…" I cleared my throat and wondered where my clever words had gone. "When I said we put the job first, I meant it. We take ourselves and our clients very seriously."

Miss Fern looked at me like she thought she knew better, but she didn't say so. "All right," was what she did say. "Good to hear."

I think we both knew that if there were any bedroom shenanigans between me and Nora, it wasn't going to be at the expense of her safety. I definitely knew it, and Miss Fern just seemed too polite to voice it out loud.

She stopped at a door. "Security hang in here when they're not needed. You'll find a few of the boys doing their thing. The others are stationed."

I gave her a nod, glad that my attraction to her bass player was now out of the spotlight. "Great. Thanks."

"I'll leave you to it. Let me know if you need anything else."

"Will do."

She left and I entered the room.

"You the new guy?" one of the guys asked.

They were all built on the Tank side of things, which meant that they were pretty much all bigger than me. They all wore black slacks and tight black t-shirts that read 'SECURITY' on them.

I nodded to the guy's t-shirt. "Subtle. I like it."

He nodded to my suit. "Poncy. I like it."

I smirked. He smirked. We were friends already.

"Anton. Head of tour security," he said, thrusting his hand towards me.

"Ryder."

Anton kicked his head to the other blokes in the room. "This here's Rico, Des and Phil."

I nodded to them in greeting. "Pleasure, fellas."

"What do you need from us?" Anton asked.

"Okay," I said, looking at the other security guys. "Talk me through a standard concert."

I didn't know if they'd had an issue when Tank had been brought in, but they seemed totally unfazed to have me there. I assumed they knew as well as I that we were there for different jobs. Their expertise was crowd control. I had plenty of experience with crowd control, but my skills were aimed more at smaller details and specific threats.

We spent some time going through the basic timeline from picking the band up from their hotel to dropping them back, whatever time and whatever state that involved. The whole thing sounded pretty standard and as expected. My job would entail being on the detail to pick Nora up, not let her out of my sight, then make sure she got back to her room and didn't leave it alone.

Simple.

Or, so I thought.

"We're going through sound check today before the concert tonight," Rico said. "Which means closed stage."

"The only people in or out have badges," Des added.

Anton passed me an ear piece. "While you're

here, you get comms. We meet an hour before the band's day starts. We go through the schedule, then break up to do pick up. I've been told you're staying in the hotel too, yes?" he asked and I nodded. "Good. So, you'll get a text when it's time to move. Just standard. Your end of day will depend heavily on Nora."

I nodded again. "So I've been told."

"The rest is take it as it comes. The band's got relative freedom and we go where the band goes."

"Okay. Can do."

"You've done this sort of job before?" Anton asked.

"VIP. Never a rockstar, though."

Anton nodded. "Pay's good. Never gets boring."

I grinned. "No. It doesn't."

I put the ear piece in. I was no stranger to the ear

piece, but it was different when you didn't have your team on the other end. It felt more like a super spy. Well, the James Bond type, not the special ops type. And, if there was one thing I'd wanted to be in my life, it was James Bond. It's why I'd joined the special ops in the first place.

Boy, were my expectations dashed.

And they'd be dashed again because the Bond thing was going to be a short-lived thing.

Suits were Tank's thing. They were Chaos' thing. They were Hawk's thing. They were my thing when Nelson was paying my wages. But I was on tour with a rockband and I'd be damned if I didn't fit in with the rest of the boys.

Fitting in meant Nora would have a little more rope, as it were.

Fitting in meant I could keep her under control by

letting her out of control.

Fitting in might also have meant bordering on 'using Nora as bait' territory. But, I'd be by her side. I'd keep her safe. So many times, these things came to nothing anyway and we were just an abundance of caution.

Tank had filled me in on every instance of the stalker's activities – all nicely encased in a structured folder – including the possible instance earlier in the week. So I was aware this situation had the potential for bodily harm.

If there was one thing the boys of Grace Grayson were ready for, it was bodily harm.

5
Nora

I wanted to know what made him tick. I wanted to know what went through his mind that he *didn't* say, given everything he did say. I wanted half an hour alone with him to find out if that tongue was really as dirty as I hoped it was.

But Adelaide gave us no chances.

Our schedule was tight. Back-to-back soundcheck and concert, then plane the next morning. None of us had time to think about family or friends we hadn't seen since moving to the States years earlier.

The closest we came to time alone was the next morning.

When he arrived at my hotel door to pick me up for the airport, the suit was gone and in its place was a pair of dark jeans and a simple long-sleeved t-shirt with the sleeves rolled up.

"When did you have time to pack a bag?" I asked him.

He grinned a delectable crocked smile. "Tank–"

"Tank?"

His smile deepened. "Gavin's nickname."

I nodded thoughtfully. "It suits."

"It does. We at Grace Grayson always have a go bag ready."

"So, you get hired and don't even have time to go

home before coming on tour with a rockband?" I teased.

He nodded faux-sorrowfully. "I know. It's a hard life. But somebody's got to do it."

"What about your girlfriend?" I asked him innocently.

He scoffed. "No girlfriend."

"Boyfriend?"

He gave me a 'touché' look. "No boyfriend, either, sadly."

"A dog?"

"Um, no," he scoffed, more indignant than before. "Definitely not a dog."

"Mother?" I suggested.

The corner of his lip tipped in humour. "I'm a big boy. I have successfully managed to move out of home and stay there, thanks."

I shrugged as I picked up my bag. "How am I supposed to know how much security makes?"

"Enough, thank you," he chuckled. "Not as much your line of work, I'll bet. But it pays the bills…and the vices."

"Good to know. Not intimidated by a woman who earns more than you, I hope."

"Not at all. Being a kept man is a dream."

"Really?" I laughed.

The eye contact was real. "Darlin', if I didn't have to work, I'd have more time to make sure my woman was always fully satisfied."

Oh, my.

Um. Yes, please.

Outside my head, I kept it a little more put together. "Good to know," I told him. "I'll keep that," I bit my lip for good measure, "in mind."

He winked and his smirk was sinfully tempting. "I know I will."

Hot dang.

Everything in me wanted to shut the door and tell Emma we'd get the next flight. Well, almost everything. There was that pesky part of me that would do anything to let the others down – i.e. missing my flight for personal gratification – and another, tiny sliver of a part that had latched onto Ryder the Kept Man idea and wanted to hold onto it, to play with it, a little longer. It wasn't going to be able to do that if I threw him into my bed the day after I'd met him.

So, on with the schedule as planned.

"We ready to move?" Anton called from further up the hallway.

"Ready," came a few calls from other rooms, and

from Ryder.

It was the same leaving any hotel. We all make this grand procession, surrounded by staff, like we were something special. Most days, I didn't feel like something special. I felt like I was doing a job, my job, which I loved.

It was humorous, then, that returning to the hotel was never the same. Sometimes we'd reverse the exit. Most of the time, we went off to parties or clubs, or the boys got a private car to take them and that night's someone back to their room. Which is not to say the boys were the only ones who did it.

"You good?" Ryder asked me and I re-focussed myself and nodded.

"Good," I told him.

"Okay."

He stuck close by as we all crowded into the

elevator. Five band members, a manager and five security guards. Strictly speaking, while we weren't above the person limit, I was pretty sure we were above the kg limit. Still, those figures were obviously cautionary because we didn't all plummet to the ground floor like stones in a sack.

The drivers had the cars ready. Not for the first time, I hated to think how long other people were waiting because the cars were always there no matter how fast or slow we were to get a move on.

Ryder held the door of the limo open for me and the boys to climb in.

We'd started taking limos more for practicality than anything else. A way we could get around and all be in one place. Easier to keep an eye on us that way. Sure, we could all have piled into an SUV, popping the third row down like we were still twelve and car-pooling on the way to a school hockey match. We could have got a van or a mini bus. But the vibe, Mabo. We were a rockband and limo was just more our vibe.

Nate, forever with his drumsticks, was whacking them on Brax's leg. "Next stop, LA!" he shouted with a wide smile.

He said it every time we headed for the airport because it was the thing he'd said when we'd moved to the States. We'd got lucky and it had become his war cry, his lucky charm. It wouldn't be a safe flight if he didn't say it.

"Get your…" Brax muttered, trying to grab the sticks from his twin.

Nate was too quick for him. "Get my what?" he asked, just begging for a bruising the rate he was going. "Get my what, Braxton?" he laughed, keeping his sticks just out of his brother's hands.

"I swear," Zach said, "We're gonna wake up and the band'll be done 'cos Brax killed him."

Cooper muttered something too low for me to hear and managed to whip Nate's sticks from him hands in one fluid motion.

"Oi!" Nate cried, all disappointment his game was over.

"Oi, yourself," Coop said. "I'll bury a body for you shits, but not if it's one of our own."

"Brax won't actually kill me," Nate said, assuredly.

"Won't I?" Brax drawled.

Nate shook his head. "Nah. That'd kill you, too."

We all looked at him in confusion.

"Freaky twin shit, eh?" he explained.

"And I suppose you feel each other's jerk-offs,

too," Coop said, miming the exact thing between his legs.

Brax and Nate looked at each other for a second like we'd discovered their greatest secret.

"Wait a second…" Zach said, leaning forward.

"Psyche!" Brax and Nate both yelled, pointing at us.

I shook my head with a smile. It wasn't often that the boys played on their whole twin thing. They usually spent more time pretending they didn't know each other at all than making jokes together or giving anyone a glimpse into their lives as not just brothers but twins. Sometimes, I was sure that only the five people in the back of that limo actually had any idea how deep the two men actually loved each other. Most of the time, I was convinced all those tiny moments of love were the joke and they actually did hate each other more than they tolerated each other.

But what was family if not one giant dysfunction?

Coop and I had always been divided by the four-year age-gap. We loved each other, we got along, but we didn't always get each other. We weren't besties and, outside music, we had no real shared passions or hobbies…unless you counted shagging groupies.

Now the boys were all in their thirties, the age-gap was becoming less noticeable. Although, I'd always considered my ovaries had given me a handicap in the maturity department and at least, in that respect, I'd always been ahead of the rest of them.

I wasn't ready for a white dress or picket fence, but I could imagine them on the horizon far more clearly than Brax, Nate, Zach or Coop. If they'd even considered the barest concept of settling down, I'd eat my guitar strings. Nup. Those guys would be bringing groupie #2,086 to my funeral.

"Tell me about this new security of yours," Nate was saying, finally over playing the drums on his brother, as he scooted over to sit next to me.

I shrugged. "Want me to put in a good word?"

Nate grinned. "That other guy's more my type."

"Gavin?"

Nate nodded. "So dreamy," he teased.

I elbowed him. "Ryder seems fine."

"Yeah, finely wrapped in those jeans."

"He's all right."

"Oh-ho!" Nate cried. "You *do* think so!"

I couldn't help looking to check the thing was up between us and the front seats.

Nate snorted. "You do, or you wouldn't have needed to know if he could hear me."

I elbowed him again, a little less gently this time. "Who I'm attracted or not attracted to is none of your business."

"I disagree." Nate flopped back against the seat and looked at me.

"I disagree with your disagreement," I told him.

"Nah, see. It is my business because it's my job to fuck up a fucker who hurts you."

I gave him a questioning look. "You think he's going to hurt me? *Me?* Do I need to remind you who you're talking to?"

"Even One-Night Nora's not immune to the mysterious ways of the heart," he said cryptically.

"You been watching one of those New Orleans specials again?" I asked him. "Macbeth?"

Nate was a history buff. Always had been. He didn't care if it was recent or before the dinosaurs, he wanted to know all about it. If there were mentions of magic, he was even more excitable. His excitement meant we heard a lot about it. It was difficult not to take some of it in.

"I'm just saying," Nate said with a shrug.

"Nothing," I told him. "You're just saying nothing."

He mimed zipping his lips and went over to annoy my brother for a change.

All the boys had their roles in the band, I guessed. To the outside world, they were all broody and moody and sexy. In the safety of our own little world, it varied. Nate was the comedian, the one who wasn't afraid to show his feelings for us, the one who tried to get us interacting as a whole. Zach was the next open, but was still withdrawn in his own little world of books in preference to socialisation. I wasn't afraid to tell the boys how I felt about them, but I never let them in on how I was feeling about myself. And it was a constant competition between Brax and Coop as to who could be the moodiest dickhead on the planet. Cooper was convinced he was the dirtier of the two, but I knew for a fact that Brax just kept his dirty for more private occasions.

Nate thankfully didn't pester me for the rest of the trip, during the wait at the airport, or the flight. It was as uneventful as it always was. Zach had his nose buried in a book. Brax practiced his guitar. Cooper went over setlists. Nate bounced around and made sure no one was bored while giving little impromptu percussion performances. He was always a hit with flight attendants.

Walking out of the airport to the waiting car had me weirdly on edge. My heart beat just a little faster and my breath caught in my throat a little more than it should have. I was vividly aware of every single noise and every single person around me.

I flinched when Nate bumped me in excitement.

I jumped when someone called my name.

Even Ryder just behind me couldn't completely assuage me. It wasn't that I thought having Gavin back would have been better or safer. Despite the way I'd behaved, I'd trusted Gavin. The problem was, I hadn't believed there'd been enough of an issue to trust him with. Now I was coming around to the problem, I was coming around to the sense in security. Even if the problem didn't amount to anything more, I was okay with caution. And I trusted Gavin enough to trust him leaving me in Ryder's hands.

"Miss Curry," Ryder said as we approached the

car.

He didn't touch me, as though he'd noticed how jumpy I was, but his arms were held out and around me in a protective and shielding position. I noticed his eyes scanning quickly around the gathered crowd.

I looked at him and he nodded to the car.

As a group, we headed towards it.

"Step back, please," Ryder said, his whole body between me and the crowd.

One woman surged towards me and I was in such a hurry to get away that I stepped on Brax's foot.

Instead of berating me or teasing me, I just felt his hands steady me.

"Don't make me ask again," Ryder said, his tone low and commanding.

For a brief moment, I hoped he was like that in

the bedroom. But I only had room for that because he'd got the crowd to back off and I could breathe properly again.

We were almost to the car. Cooper and Brax were in. Nate was getting in.

"Would fucking listen to Tank," I heard Ryder mutter.

"You kiss your mother with that mouth?" I teased as Zach climbed into the car.

He gave me a soft lop-sided smile. "You weren't supposed to hear that."

"That's not an answer to my question."

This time, it was a devilish crooked grin. "You'll find I don't mix family and pleasure, Miss Curry," he said matter-of-fact.

I liked the sound of that. I kicked my chin towards him. "You want to stay less conspicuous? You'd better start calling me Nora," I said before I swung into the waiting car and pulled the door closed behind me.

6
Ryder

"Status report?" Chaos said as he picked up the call.

"Well hello to you, too, fine sir," I said, faking the indignance.

"You've been missed," he told me, more to placate me than anything else, I was sure. "How are things?"

"Good," I said, looking over to where Nora was signing merchandise with the boys in preparation for their meet and greet the next day.

We'd flown into our first stop the day before and then been hanging out at the hotel around soundcheck. The night before at the hotel had been uneventful. I'd left Nora in her room, which was next to mine with an adjoining door, and she'd still been there the next morning. Overnight, I'd checked up on her until the second time I'd woken her up and deemed her not likely going anywhere.

"I've seen the pictures," Chaos said.

I couldn't quite tell from his tone whether that was good or bad.

"You look like you're fitting in," he finished and I breathed a sigh of relief.

I was a confident man, bordering on arrogant. I thought I was top shit at the things I did and avoided the stuff I knew I sucked at. I knew I was good at my job. I knew I could get done whatever needed doing.

But, when your boss agrees with you, it feels good. Not going to lie. A mark of the arrogant was the desperate need for validation, especially when I knew I wasn't the first pick for the gig.

For all my epically good traits – or flaws, if you listened to Nico – I knew who and what I was. I liked shiny things. I got excited about VIPs. I wanted the famous people jobs. I didn't want fame, but rubbing shoulders was always fun. Being able to dip my toe into their world and not commit anything was the ultimate in experiences.

"I figured the job called for something a little more laid back," I said. "Tank parading around in his suit like he's protecting the president, or Falkner."

Chaos laughed roughly. "You can do the job differently without it being wrong."

"Isn't that just what I said?" I asked with a grin.

"How's it actually going?"

I nodded. "Fine. No sign of her trying to give me the slip–"

"What about you giving her the slip?" Chaos butted in.

"I don't know what you're talking about," I said, pretending to be offended.

"Tank told me you two had…chemistry."

"I'll bet he did, the devil. You tell him that, if he wants this booty, he's gotta put a ring on it first. I'm *just* not that kind of boy."

"The hell you're not," he muttered, and I heard the smile in his voice. "You and Miss Curry, Rollie…" he said when I didn't offer any more information.

"Strictly profesh, bossman. Swear on my life."

"And how long's that going to last?"

I couldn't help grinning. "You going to reassign me, too?"

"Not if you get the job done. But, Rollie…"

I nodded. "I know, mate. Job first. You know I know."

"I know. But I like to check. It's not your name on the building."

"Well, no. My name'd make us sound like some kind of lawyers or something."

"You'd also have to be more mature."

I crossed myself, even knowing Chaos couldn't see me. "Say it isn't so."

"Nico would blow us all before letting your name on the building."

"Oh, Chaos, behave," I teased.

"I walked into that one."

"Rookie mistake. Hate to see it."

"You try running a company and see how well your brain works."

"You seemed fine before you had Bert to get home to."

"What are you saying about my relationship?"

I shrugged. "Nah, I think it looks good on you. We could all stand to have more than just the job to keep us warm at night."

"Rollie, you ok–?"

"I'd best go. Shit security spend all day on their phones. I'll check in again in a couple of days."

"All right–"

I hung up on him and shoved my phone in my pocket.

We could all do with more than the job to keep us warm at night, I'd stand by that statement. I wasn't ashamed of it. I'd tell anyone who wanted to know.

But that didn't mean I wanted to talk about it beyond the statement. It didn't need explaining.

What did need explaining was why I looked at Nora while I was thinking about it.

"Because I'm doing my job," I told myself. "Not because I'm open to the idea of my first serious relationship being with someone who lives on the other side of the world."

And I'd be damned if I didn't believe it.

"Oi, Ryder," Nate called to me.

"Yeah?" I asked as I went over.

He held a t-shirt up towards me. "What size are you?"

"Bit personal," I joked and he laughed.

I liked Nate. He reminded me a bit of Hawk when Hawk was being easily led along on my shenanigans. He had the humour. He had the timing. He knew how to diffuse or lighten a situation with a bit of good old comic relief. Actually, thinking about it, he was the me of *Valjean*.

"Nah," I said. "Medium, usually. Why?"

Nate held up one hand as he wrote on a t-shirt with the other. Finally, he picked up the shirt and showed me his handiwork.

In big red letters across the *Valjean* branding he'd written 'Nora ♡'s Ryder'.

I spat a laugh and Nora huffed.

"Grow up, Nate!" she said, rolling her eyes.

"Is it a shirt of lies?" Nate smirked.

I pointed at him. "Loved *Despicable Me*!"

"It was so good, eh?" Nate grinned.

"Are there two of them now? Is that what's happening?" Miss Fern sighed.

I shrugged. "I babysit. I don't know what his

excuse is."

"He's a child," Nora said.

"Only on the inside!" Nate said, quite proudly and I snorted.

Nora stood up. "I'm done. I need a drink. I suppose a club is out of the question?" she asked me, totally resigned and ready for me to say no.

But that wasn't the new plan. "Not at all."

Everyone looked at me then.

"Wait on," Nate said. "If Nora's going clubbing, I want to go, too."

"Have you finished your homework?" Brax asked him.

Nate stuck his tongue out at him. "Yes, Mum." He threw the t-shirt he'd just 'signed' to me. "Here you go, mate. On the house."

I looked at Nora over the offending item of

clothing and smirked. She smirked back.

"Hell, if I'm allowed clubbing, I'll wear it," she said.

Nate was hurriedly making his way through a stack of photo posters. "Not without me, you're not."

"Meet and Greet starts at eight, *ladies*…" Miss Fern said, half-reminder and half-warning.

I winked at her. "Consider them pumpkins. Home by two."

"I think you'll find it was midnight." But Miss Fern smiled.

"I'm getting my bag," Nora said.

Brax, Zach and Cooper decided to go their own way for the night, so that left Nora and Nate going out clubbing. I coordinated with the other security detail about protocol and Anton said he'd come along with me.

Nate took Anton's chin in his hand. "Oh, a fella's gotta get *drunk* to kiss this mug." Then he winked and patted Anton's cheek. "Or does he?" And sauntered off towards the elevator.

I looked to Nora, who was not going to give me any explanation as to what I just watched, then to Anton, who was a little more forthcoming as Nora followed Nate out.

"Nate likes to think he shocks people," Anton said as we, in turn, followed the others.

"And I thought *I* liked to shock people."

Anton shrugged. "Be interesting to see if he still made those jokes if he knew I was gay."

"You think he wouldn't?"

Anton gave me a smile. "On the contrary, I think he would."

And this was one of the things I loved about my

job. Not only did I get to meet sexy women like Nora, but I met different people and groups with different dynamics and I got to watch how they all interacted. I got to see what their in-jokes were. I got to experience a little bit of their lives.

The cynic in me would say I enjoyed experiencing other people's lives because it let me avoid experiencing my own. And, maybe that was true. But, I figured, as far as coping mechanisms went, it could have been worse. Like I'd said to Bert on that first Champers Day, all of us could have had worse coping mechanisms.

Nate directed us to a club and the driver pulled up outside. Anton had given the run down of his protocols for when we got inside. I, of course, had different directions.

As Anton hung back and kept watch from a

respectable distance, I kept up with Nora and Nate. If either of them thought it was weird, they didn't say anything. The four of us were let into the VIP section and drinks were ordered.

"Anton, my man!" Nate called. "Shots!"

Anton merely shook his head once and went back to pretending he wasn't there.

"Ryder?" Nora said, the very coaxing nature of her voice making me stand to attention.

"Miss Curry?"

"What did I say about that?" she chastised.

"Nora?" I amended.

"Better. Shot?"

I nodded. "Why not."

Drinks flowed freely and even I was glad I didn't have to pay. I measured myself, made sure I paced myself. That was what I was here to do after all. Let

Nora lose control and be right beside to make sure she stayed safe.

At some point, Nate caught the eye of – in his words – a pretty young thing, and went off to do what Nate Glenn did best. Which left Nora and me sitting on the lounge over a tray of shots.

"This the new plan then?" she asked over the music.

"What?" I asked as I finished my drink.

"You get me drunk and I might sleep with you?"

I grinned. "I don't need or want you drunk for that."

"You seem to have a very high opinion of yourself."

I grinned. "Someone has to."

She looked me up and down. "Do you dance, Ryder?"

I nodded. "I've been known to."

She held her hand out and I took it.

"Good," she said. "Dance with me."

She dragged me back downstairs and onto the dancefloor, not afraid to get her body up close and personal with mine. Her arm wound around my neck as she swayed to the music. And all the while, her eyes were pinned to mine like it was some sort of challenge. I didn't know exactly what it was, but I was more than happy to meet it.

"You got something in your pocket, or just happy to see me?" she asked me, pressing her leg between mine.

"If I said it was something in my pocket?"

"Then, I might be disappointed," she purred in my ear and I was momentarily convinced I could fall in love with her right there.

I was beginning to think it was a good thing nothing had happened about this attraction we had. If we'd jumped into bed that first night, I might not have been getting to know her so well. I might have taken a different approach to her safety and I quite liked what we had going on.

I was going to need one hell of a cold shower when we got back to the hotel, but I could handle that.

7
Nora

My initial fear and anxiety were easing. It had been over two weeks of not seeing or hearing anything weird or freaky or chilling, and I was beginning to think that Ryder was right; it had been opportunity, a once-off.

There'd been nothing in Adelaide and there was nothing here except the same thing I'd seen for the last five years of our careers; general fans doing typical, harmless fan things.

We'd got through the Meet and Greet – a whole day of lines and lines of people wanting autographs and pictures and voicemail messages. Who even used voicemail anymore? I'd felt apprehensive at the beginning. As time had gone on, though, and no one did anything more than the usual gushing over how much they loved me and *Valjean* and our music, I'd relaxed fully. This was the life I knew. I could navigate this seamlessly.

Ryder was there through it all, faded into the background like all the other security, but never out of sight. He was like a beacon of safety in a sea of potential uncertainty. Which gave me conflicting feelings after the previous night.

He wasn't the first security guard I'd danced with. He wasn't the first security guard to get a boner while we were dancing – alright, while I was rubbing my body up against theirs. He was, though, the first security guard whose boner had got me excited. To that degree anyway.

I'd wanted nothing more than to pull him close and kiss him like my life depended on it. I'd wanted to see what he tasted like right there on the dancefloor. I didn't care if a million people saw us. I didn't care if it got plastered all over the news. I wanted him more than all of that.

Or, did I?

Because I hadn't done anything.

And it wasn't just the worry that people might get the wrong idea about us if they saw. I'd partied with plenty of people I'd slept with and there'd been pictures all over the net without speculation I was about to slip into a big white dress or anything.

I had to admit to myself that there was a tiny part

of me who didn't want to share him. To share our moment. I'd wanted our moment – if we had a moment – to be just between us. I wanted to keep something – I wanted to keep him – to myself for once.

But he was making that idea very difficult as we took a break and Ryder came over to me as I was getting a drink.

"How's it going?" he asked.

I shrugged and shook out my hand. We might have spent a huge portion of the day before signing stuff, but there was always more to sign.

"Fine. Good. I need to get a new stack of pens, though."

He gave me that crocked smile. The one that made his green eyes sparkle and made my stomach knot.

"I meant, anything out there that's worrying you?

Are you comfortable?" he asked.

"There is one guy who keeps staring at me..." I started and I saw Ryder snap to attention. "He's been over in the corner wearing this dark ball cap, dark jeans, and this cheesy Ramones t-shirt."

He'd obviously been taking it in, making himself a mental picture...then stopped and looked down at his chest.

"Very funny," he said, but his lips were fighting a smile.

"What? You stare at me *a lot*, know what I'm saying?"

"It's my job," he told me.

I shrugged. "Whatever. You can admit you like me, you know."

"Oh, *I* can admit it?" he laughed.

I nodded. "You wouldn't be the first."

"From what I hear, it'd be a first for you to admit it."

I smirked. "Admit what?"

"That you like me."

"Do I like you?" I asked innocently, knowing exactly what the answer was to that.

"Nora Curry, you *wish* you knew how good we'd be together."

"Oh, do I?"

He nodded. "Oh, yeah."

"You think *you* know?"

He tapped the side of his head. "I don't just keep potential creeps up here, you know."

"What exactly do you keep up there?"

"Well," he started as though he was about to launch into a full description. "It just wouldn't be appropriate for me say any more. On account of how you don't like me and all."

Did he just...? Was he actually going to pretend like he was some gentleman who wasn't going to tell me in full explicit detail exactly what he wanted to do to me when I had *just* asked him to? Was he really going to play the 'Oh, you're not interested' card? Did this guy have more game than I had originally suspected him of having?

It seemed he did.

"Nora?" Emma called. "Time."

I didn't know what to say to Ryder. My mouth hung open uselessly for a moment as I tried to pull words into a sentence. The wittier the better. But nothing came.

"You just keep your eyes on me, buddy," was all I came up with.

"Wouldn't dream of looking anywhere else," he

replied.

I felt a little flush as I walked back to my seat.

Emma had done her job, though, and there was another set of my signing pens waiting for me. I just wished I could say I paid attention to what I did with them. I didn't, I kept looking at Ryder.

How could a guy just stand in a corner and look sexy?

Like the other guys, he had his hands behind his back and his legs were parted a little. Even from that distance, I could see the cheekiness on his face. I could picture the twinkle in his eye as he watched me sign paper after poster after shirt after book. Now and then, his eyes left me and scanned the crowd. But it wasn't long until they were back on me again.

And I wanted more than his eyes on me.

In Ryder, I felt like I'd found a kindred spirit.

There was a connection. A spark. From the moment I first saw him, it felt like we shared a secret. I didn't know what that secret was, though. It was like he knew me, knew who I was, and I knew him. Or, better yet, he wanted to know me and I wanted to know him. I hadn't felt that since my last crush back in my teens.

I was caught between fantasies. I kept picturing dragging him into my hotel room and crushing my lips to his. But I also pictured pulling two beers out of the fridge and sitting down to chat with him over drinks that weren't hampered by loud club music.

Mostly, it was the kissing thing. But every so often, it was the talking thing. Both of which totally threw me off my game.

"Where have you been all morning?" Coop asked me at lunch.

I blinked. "What do you mean?"

He kicked his head towards the conference room where there were still crowds of people waiting for us to come back.

"You've just been going through the motions." He looked around. "Are you worried about the stalker?"

It felt like the first time that day I was being totally honest about something. "No. We haven't seen any more about him for, like, weeks."

"It was Tokyo, two weeks ago."

"What? Are you a clock now?" I huffed, thinking it was perfectly my luck that the one time my brother can keep his own time was when I'd rather he didn't.

"I'm a concerned older brother who has to look out for his sister because she won't do it for herself."

I pointed to Ryder. "That's what Emma pays him

for."

"Yeah," Cooper huffed a humourless laugh. "You get how thankless my job is now? And I'm stuck with it for life."

"No one asked you to care," I grumbled.

"No," he agreed, taking my chin in my hands and making me look at him. "But I can hardly help it when I've got a sister like you."

It was the mushiest we ever got with each other. Maybe we should have been mushier. Maybe we should have said we loved each other more often. But we knew. When you saw your brother every day, you didn't need to tell him. He knew. Likewise, you knew he loved you. It was in all the teasing. It was in all the digs. It was even in all the fights.

I gave Coop a nod. "Yeah. Well, I had a good role model."

"If you say Brax, I'll never speak to you again," he said with a wry grin.

I shoved him. "Go away," I told him, not wanting to ruin the moment but not wanting it to go any deeper.

He left me and was replaced by Ryder with a bottle of water he held out towards me.

"Drink?" he asked.

As I took it from him, our fingers brushed and I felt my heart flutter excitedly in my chest. I looked at him and I saw the mischief in his eyes. I saw the answering interest. We stood there, for too long, both holding the water bottle between us. Neither of us interested in pulling away or breaking the connection we had.

"All right, people, five minutes," Emma called. "Spit, swallow, cover it up. I don't care, but be public-ready in five. You hear me Brax?"

"Yeah, yeah," he muttered as he walked out. "Five minutes. Keep your knickers on."

I gently tugged the water bottle towards me and Ryder finally let go of it.

"Thanks," I said, holding it up.

He nodded. "No worries."

"I didn't realise catering was part of security's job."

His eyes were all smoulder. His mouth was all supple possibility. His words were all dripping in velvet.

"My job is very…diverse."

"That must be hard."

He shook his head. "Not at all. It's quite simple really."

"How so?"

"It's all about satisfaction. And my job is to satisfy you, Nora Curry."

Did I really have to go back to adoring fans for the next six hours?

Needing to swallow hard, I covered by taking a sip of the water and nodded. "So far, so good."

"Yeah?"

I nodded again as I raked my eyes down and up his body. "So far."

As I walked away, I added a little more sway to my hips, knowing he'd be watching. It was easy in my heels, the great big things that had become part of my brand that I took too much pleasure kicking off at the end of the night.

Leaving things the way we did, I felt like I had the upper hand. I felt like the one in control of whatever back and forth we were doing. So, I could take him watching me for six hours. I could take the heated look he gave me or the mischievous grin he flashed now and then.

I could take it the rest of the way through the Meet and Greet and then back up to my room.

"All right, you let me know if you need anything else tonight, ma'am," Ryder said with his easy cheek.

There was one thing I needed from him.

"Ryder…" I said as he made to walk out, my hand on his arm.

He looked back at me, his eyebrow raised in questioning anticipation. "Yeah?"

I hooked my finger in his jeans waistband and pulled him towards me. "Don't leave."

Ryder's eyes searched mine as the corner of his lip tipped in a crooked grin. "Do you like me or something?" he teased.

"I want you…or something," I told him.

He nodded like he was thinking. "I can go with that."

He kicked the door closed behind him and took a step towards me. One hand went to my cheek and the other to my waist as he took another step. Without hesitation, he dipped his head and caught me in a breathtaking kiss. It didn't take my breath away because it was savage passion. Quite the opposite. It was soft and earnest. It surprised me. It felt like it surprised him, too.

Suddenly, everything changed and there was that passion. Our kiss deepened and our hands couldn't get enough of each other's bodies. It was like they had to search every inch, sear it into memory. My arms wound around his neck and my fingers slid into his hair.

He overwhelmed my senses. His smell enveloped me in a bubble of warm spices and something tangy I wanted to lick. His body was hot and hard against mine.

He pushed me up against the wall and my body wrapped around his. I wondered in the sense of it in the same thought that I berated myself for waiting so long – because a couple of days was *so long*. How could I want something so badly and hesitate about it so strongly? But the want won out. Oh, how the want won out.

As he kissed me, his hand slipped between my legs and he ran his fingers over me gently. It was enough sensation to ignite desperate need while not being nearly enough, and my hips rocked towards him. I felt like my whole body was hypersensitive to anywhere we touched; our lips, shoulders, chest, legs. I felt like I'd never get him close enough to me. I needed more. Oh, so much more of him.

I felt Ryder smile against my lips. He liked what he was doing to me. I would have been indignant had I not liked it too; I hadn't felt want – no, need – like this is possibly ever.

Ryder's hand was less teasing now as he rubbed me over my jeans. But it was just the warm up and I wanted the main event. My hips rocked into his hand again and, like we were on the same wavelength, he seemed to know what I wanted.

He deftly undid my jeans and slid his hand, in one fluid motion, down under my undies. I gasped against him as bare skin met bare skin and it felt better than I'd even thought it would.

The chuckle of unsurprised pride that vibrated

through him didn't make me feel embarrassed or dominated. If he kept making me feel as good as he was, I didn't care how arrogant he was. Arrogance had a place in the bedroom and I was very happy to benefit from it.

As his lips trailed to my neck, Ryder's fingers worked me like he could read exactly what I wanted when I wanted it. His touch moved in perfect sync with my body. Even with the awkward angle we'd found ourselves in.

I could only hold onto him tightly as the pleasure built to a crescendo. I gave a breathy moan as he brought me to orgasm and pulled his lips back to mine. As he rubbed me slower and I rode the wave back down, I kissed him hard, ignoring the need to get my breath back and just wanting to stay in that feeling for as long as possible.

Finally, the aftershocks wore down to gentle waves and my head fell back against the wall as I breathed out deeply and gave a chuckle of satisfaction.

8
Ryder

"Not bad," she said, looking at me with a twinkle of mischief in her eyes.

"Oh, just not bad?" I asked.

She shrugged nonchalantly, then laughed as I pulled her towards me. She kissed me lazily as she started walked me back towards the bed.

"You want more, do you?" I said.

"I want all of you," she said as she went for my jeans button.

I pulled off my t-shirt and threw it on the floor. "Your wish is my command."

All jokes were put aside as there was disrobing to finish. There was skin to kiss. There was body to touch.

We didn't talk.

A sudden almost seriousness had fallen over us. Not serious. Focussed.

We had a mission and we weren't going to let anything distract us from it.

When we were both naked, I picked her up and lay her on the bed, settling between her legs. Her knee came up and hugged my hip and I couldn't wait to be inside her. To distract myself, I peppered her in kisses and she laughed as her arms wrapped around me tighter.

"Wait, wait!" she said, still laughing.

I pulled away quickly.

She looked at me weirdly. "You okay?"

I nodded. "You said wait."

"I said wait, not get your clothes on and get out. I'm just getting a condom." She shook her head with a smile and reached over to the floor where she'd thrown her bag.

I dropped back on the bed. "Sorry. Force of habit."

"You get stopped halfway a lot?" she asked.

I smirked as she crawled over to me. "No. I'm just big into consent."

She straddled my legs. "Good to know," she said as she ripped open the condom and started rolling it onto me.

I watched her appreciatively. I usually tried to get this bit over with as quickly as possible. Nothing ruined the mood quite like pausing for health and safety reasons. But Nora ran her hands over my shaft slowly as she made sure the condom was on properly and I began to appreciate there was a way to make health and safety fun and cool.

When she seemed satisfied it was on, she lowered herself over me and kissed me while she lined me up. My hands on her hips were not the driving force behind me sliding into her slowly, but they felt they needed to be there for moral support.

Letting her be in charge wasn't new to me, but I'd never given over control without it being a game of some sort. This didn't feel like a game. This felt like sharing. My first instinct was to leap out of bed and run away, but then she started to move on me and I was a goner.

She started out slow, her pace gently increasing

until she was riding me hard and fast. She sat up and I just watched her in awed admiration as she took what she wanted how she wanted it. Her rhythm slowed ever so slightly as her orgasm mounted again and it gave me insurmountable pleasure to watch hers spread across her face.

After it passed, Nora rolled us over so I was on top of her and she gave me a sinful smirk and grabbed one of my arse cheek in her hands.

"Your turn," she said.

"Oh, I think you've got more in you," I sassed.

Her eyes were all humour. "Maybe, but," she reached up and her lips stroked my ear as she said, "I want you to take me, Ryder. Hard. Fast. No mercy."

Well, who was I to deny a goddess what she wanted?

I slid my hand down her leg and coaxed it higher around my hip, giving me full access to her. I dropped my lips to her jaw, her neck, her collarbone and started thrusting. Much like she had, I started slow, working my way up to pace.

Her hands gripped me, one on my back and one on my arse as she moved with me.

She filled my senses and I felt like I was drunk on her.

Her scent was sweetly at odds with her personality; floral and berries.

She was gorgeous to me, yeah, but it was that personality – that sass – that fired me up to the point of madness. We'd only known each other a few days and yet I knew she was one of my kind. I knew we just fit. We worked.

And not just her body and mine, although they

went together incredibly complimentarily as well. It got me excited. She got me excited.

She wanted no mercy? She'd get it.

We moved together, we breathed together, we moaned wordless encouragements together until she came a third time and it sent me over the edge to join her.

Our pace slowed as we got our breaths back slowly.

Eventually, though, health and safety interrupted the mood once again, but I wasn't about to leave her side for long. I dropped back on the bed next to her, still breathing heavily.

As we lay there, in no particular hurry to go anywhere, she ran her hands over the ink on my body.

"How many girls have you slept with who have

more tattoos than you?" she asked me.

I laughed. "Not many, admittedly."

"Okay, what's this one?" She ran her hand over the one on my pec.

I took her hand and held it over the sword and starburst. "My team got that one when our commander died," I told her, looking at her with a soft smile.

"That's sweet," she said. "This one?"

I looked down at my shoulder. "I lost a bet," I said as I laughed at the memory. "Hawk bet me I couldn't chew a whole packet of Mentos sour gum at once. I was young and naïve, full of the confidence of youth. I got about halfway before my mouth reached maximum sour capacity. The next day, I had an appointment to be plastered by a giant hawk for all time."

"What was he getting if you won?"

"I hadn't settled yet on my name in a heart or Nico's suggestion which was 'Rollie is Awesome' in Doctor Who circle language."

"Rollie?" she asked.

I nodded. "As Gavin is Tank, so I am Rollie."

"Okay, I get Tank, but why Rollie?"

"In my dark and shady past, I was known to have a little thing for rollies."

"Rollies? You mean Rollos? Those little caramel chocolates?"

I snorted. "No. Like smokes. The hand-rolled ones."

"Ah." She nodded and went back to looking at my ink. "What about this one?" she asked, trying to sound out the Latin on my ribs.

"'By the Grace of Chaos'," I translated.

"What's that mean?"

"Chaos, Kit Grayson, is our esteemed leader. Grace is for Hawk– Patrick Grace. It's because of them that those of us who got home safe did so. It's because Chaos saved us all. And mostly so he could get Hawk home to his sister."

"Not, then, because they order you around?" she asked, thankfully lightening the mood like she knew that's what I needed.

"I was under the impression *you* told me what to do," I told her ruefully.

Nora laughed and covered her head with the blanket.

She looked so free and easy, there in bed with me, and I felt a little bubble well in my chest pleasantly.

It was new and it was different. It was a feeling I almost instantly pushed away; unused to peace as I was. But I tried to take a leaf out of my mates' books and let it be. As I did, something became very clear to me.

Nora Curry may have thought this was another one of the one-night stands that gave her her nickname, but I didn't agree. I was damn sure I'd do what it took to show her how good it could be again.

Fuck it, I'd woo the girl if I had to.

9
Nora

The next leg of the tour. Four more to go.

I loved travel, but the constant start-stop and packing and unpacking was starting to wear thin. My little apartment back in the States was feeling awful inviting just then.

As was the look in Ryder's eyes whenever I looked at him.

We'd stayed in bed that whole night. Not all of it was sex – though, there was quite a bit of that, too.

We talked and laughed, comparing tattoos and backstories and crazy tales from our pasts. It had been great. All of it.

It called to me, refusing to leave me alone, demanding more.

More that I knew Ryder was happy to give.

More than I knew Ryder wanted as much as I did.

But I was One-Night Nora. I couldn't do more. I couldn't do again. My reputation was all I had. If I lost it, what else would I lose? Anything I *might* gain just couldn't stack up to the everything that *was* at stake.

So, I didn't invite him to stay, no matter how much I wanted to, and he didn't ask.

It made me want him even more, just the amount of not pushing he did. He was still flirty, he was still suggestive, but never once did he try and make a move. He didn't make any assumptions that what had happened once would happen again. I appreciated it, but part of me also wished he would make a move, just so I could give in.

So, it was probably good timing that what happened next happened when it did.

As Ryder and I walked into my dressing room that night, we found the usual flowers and presents spread around that people had sent. As far as I knew, not everything made it to the dressing rooms; we were sent a lot of stuff that there just wasn't space for.

"Oh," I said as I saw a rectangular-shaped gift, all wrapped up nicely. "This had better be chocolate. I could really go for chocolate right now."

"I could just get you some chocolate," Ryder said.

"You could. But why bother when they are just

here?"

I opened the paper. There weren't chocolates inside. It was a picture frame. A really thick picture frame. Inside was a picture I didn't understand. I turned it over and looked at the back of it. There was nothing there to explain it. There wasn't an explanation anywhere.

"That's weird," I said.

"What's weird?" Brax asked as he walked in.

"This picture," I told him, holding it up.

He shrugged and went over to my make up bag.

"You right?" I asked him.

He nodded. "Eyeliner. The shit this makeup dude has is crap. It's going to run like fuck." He nodded to Ryder. "Hey, man."

Ryder nodded back.

We alternated between makeup artists and doing

it ourselves. Depended on the venue and our schedules. So, we always had a makeup bag with us. At least, I always had a makeup bag with me. Brax never carted anything around if he didn't have to.

I left him to it. Brax had been guylining since his emo days in high school. Not that he'd admit that to anyone else. And not that it was just him, all the boys had experimented back in the day. I still had the pictures squirrelled away at my parents' place to prove it should it ever need proving.

"What is it, though?" I asked, looking at the picture again.

"Dunno. Something arty?" Ryder guessed. "Looks familiar, but I don't know where from."

"What's happening? What did I miss?" I heard Zach ask as he appeared in the doorway. "And why has Nora got the emblem from *Catching Fire* framed?"

We all looked at him, standing oblivious in the doorway.

"The what?" Ryder asked.

Zach looked around at everyone like it was obvious. "*Catching Fire*. You know the whole mockingjay thing with the fires of rebell…" He petered to a stop, his eyes darting between the picture and me.

"What, Zach?" I asked. "I don't like the way you stopped talking."

"Fire…" he muttered like he was thinking. "Mockingjay…bird. Fire…bird." He looked dead at me. "*Firebird*."

With a shout, I smacked the picture off the table. "Seriously?" I snapped.

It was bad enough the stalker had claimed my

song to torment me with. But most of that was online and I made sure to avoid it. This, though? Sending me pictures and hiding in alleys in case I go there to sing at me were a whole other level of shit.

Firebird was one of our most successful songs. I'd been scared shitless when we'd released it into the world. It was so different from our usual stuff, not in the least because I'd taken lead. But they'd loved it. The fans had loved it. They'd rallied around it and supported it with everything they had. It was fast becoming one of our most played songs on all the streaming platforms.

So, for this wanker to come along and try to take that from me or ruin it for me was more than insulting.

"Where does he get off?" I muttered.

"You don't want to know," Ryder said.

I looked at him. Gone was all hint of flirtation or mischief. In its place was a guy doing a job. He was serious and calculating and ready for anything. I was pretty sure Zach could throw something at him completely from left field and Ryder'd catch it.

I saw him touch a finger to his ear. "Anyone had a visual on a package wrapped in pink, sparkly paper headed for Nora's room?" he asked.

Zach looked like he was about to answer him when he realised Ryder had been speaking into the ear piece dangling from his ear.

"Did I ever mention liking the Hunger Games?" I asked no one in particular while Ryder talked to the guys on the other end of the ear piece.

"Not that I remember," Zach said.

"Pretty obscure reference, then."

"It was probably mentioned in an interview

sometime," Brax drawled, busying applying more eyeliner to the already decent amount around his eyes.

"You right, man?" I asked him.

He stood up and looked at me. "Yes. Why?"

"You're channelling the spirits of *all* the emo that came before."

"Ha!" he barked a short laugh, then was deadpan again. "So funny." He dropped my eyeliner back into my makeup bag and stalked out.

"Nice to know you care about my safety," I sang out the door to him.

"Nice to know your hired muscle could do more damage than I could," he sang back, his voice receding as he did.

"No one remembers seeing it," Ryder said, stepping over to me and Zach.

"Maybe I'm just reading into it?" Zach said.

"If Nora's not known for an enduring love of the Hunger Games, then it's probably not a ridiculous assumption to make," Ryder replied.

I shrugged. "The movies were…fine. I never read the books."

Ryder looked at me. "You're okay?"

I nodded. "I'm annoyed, but I'm fine."

"You're good to still go on tonight?" Zach asked.

I nodded. "I'm fine. I promise I'm fine. A little light stalking isn't going to stop me from living my life!"

Ryder looked at me like he was impressed with me. Had I not just received the diversion I had, I might have looked closer at that. I might have had time for notions of, maybe not romance, but interactions of an amorous nature.

As it was, the diversion couldn't have come at a better time.

Now there was no need to tell either of us that what had happened between us was a one-time thing. There was no reason to avoid talking about it because there was something else that needed our attention. There was no reason for awkwardness or lingering questions.

I was going to get on with my life. Both in regards to the stalker and Ryder.

I was a strong independent woman who wasn't about to let a man get in the way of her living her best life. I wasn't going to let the stalker put me off my love for the music. And I wasn't going to let Ryder knock me off balance with his mischievous bedroom eyes and tempting smile.

No matter how much I might want to have a second round with them.

10
Ryder

Spending the night with Nora hadn't made me forget my job. I was a Grace Grayson boy at heart and the job was all.

The fact the job involved Nora didn't distract me from it. It made it more personal.

It was a dangerous line I was treading.

I knew the job should never be personal.

With Nora, I couldn't help it.

She was all I thought about.

When she was signing whatever a fan thrust in front of her.

When she was posing for a camera.

When she was on stage performing.

When she was in her room next door. So close, but so far away.

Her body had drawn me in, but her mind and her mouth kept me hooked.

I wanted another night with her. Badly. I couldn't remember the last time I'd wanted anything more than I wanted just one more night with her. Even if that was all I'd ever get. Even if all we did was throw back a few beers and talk more about our awkward teen years. I just wanted one more night when it was her and me against the world.

But she was saying no.

One-Night Nora was sticking to her moniker.

That was fine. The world didn't revolve around me. At the moment, it seemed to revolve around her. And I just had to be thankful that while she wasn't going to bed with me at least she wasn't going to bed with anyone else either.

"I don't know if I want room service or to go clubbing," she said to me as we walked back to her hotel room after an interview in the conference room.

"Are you asking my opinion, or thinking out loud?" I asked.

She threw me a smile. "Can it be both?"

I grinned. "Those are two very different activities," I said as I swiped her door card over the lock.

As I opened the door, I gave the room a cursory sweep, then held it open for her to enter.

"Always the gentleman," she said cheerfully.

"I think you'll find it's tactical," I answered cheekily.

"Oh?"

I nodded as I did a sweep of the bathroom. "It gives me a chance to check the room's safe before you enter it."

"So, not you being polite, then?"

"Can it be both?" I asked with a wink.

"I guess it can." She sat on the bed and started pulling her shoes off. "Is that something you learned? Like special security school? Or does it just come naturally?"

I laughed. "Security school? I wish. A chunk of it was basic training. Quite a bit of it is common sense. A lot of it was learning on the job."

"How much call does Adelaide have for stalker

threats?"

"Yeah. Not much. Most of Grace Grayson's gigs are escorting high flyer's wives to events they don't want to go to. We do a bit of general security for companies, but most of it is to make people look good in certain situations."

"Then where did you learn all your safety stuff."

"Military."

She nodded. "Your commander. The Grace of Chaos." She looked at me to confirm she had it right.

I nodded. "Yup. We were all in the military together. We all moved to Adelaide with Chaos and Hawk to work for them when we retired. A civ life without the boys seemed a little too…daunting, so Tank, Nico and I all jumped at it. No questions."

Daunting was putting it mildly. The idea of being without my team on a daily basis after barely seeing the back of them for five years was more than daunting. It was terrifying. The idea of going back home made it feel like it'd just erase the previous years, leaving me with nothing but the bad memories and the trauma. At least this way, we could surround ourselves with people who got it.

"You're not from Adelaide originally?"

I shook my head. "Country Victoria boy, me."

She snorted. "What? Like a farm?"

I nodded. "Like a farm, but not quite a farm. Just the middle of nowhere."

"Wow. I can't picture that."

"Me either. Anymore. I'm not sure even me mum would recognise me these days," I said, totally making the whole situation more real.

I hadn't meant to do it. Not consciously. I just couldn't help this concept that had been pattering about my head lately; the concept of finding more with someone. Maybe Nora wasn't the right someone. Maybe I was still too fucked up even for a cat. But how would I know if I didn't give it a try?

Nora could be the right someone. I refused to deny the potential. I could talk to her. I wanted to talk to her. I was attracted to her, mentally and physically. The rest I could discover in time. Including our compatibility, or lack of.

"The military was hard?" she asked.

I'd thought she'd run away from the realness, not lean into it.

"No harder than anyone else's service, I'm sure. But I walked away more fucked up than I went in."

"Life has a way of…" She stopped like she was lost for words.

"Changing you?" I suggested.

She nodded. "Changing you," she agreed.

The moment kind of stagnated there and it felt a lot like I'd ruined it.

"So," I said more jovially. "Decided between room service and clubbing?"

She nodded, seeming distracted by her thoughts. "Room service, I think."

"Okay. Well, you let me know if you change your mind. I'll be in my room." Kicking myself for being too vulnerable and needy and desperate, and ruining the rapport I had with this awesome woman.

She got up to walk me to the door – all of two steps away. "'Night, Ryder."

"'Night, Nora."

I opened the door and, as she went to take it from me, our hands brushed. Her eyes darted up to mine and she bit her lip.

Something palpable zinged between us. I saw it in her eyes. I felt it in the tension of our bodies, like we couldn't decide if we wanted to surge forward and rip each other's clothes off or run screaming in the other direction.

She didn't say anything. She didn't ask to me to stay. She didn't ask me to leave. I went with the safer route and decided leaving was best. I didn't want her chasing me or anything; I was fucked up, but not that badly. I just wanted whatever happened between us to be on her schedule. The ball was in her court.

I gave her a nod and walked back to my room.

Once in there, I reached for my phone and decided Chaos was probably due an update.

As the call rang, I fell back onto the bed and tried chasing images of gorgeous red heads from my mind.

"Kit Grayson," he finally answered.

"Ryder Andrews," I said, mimicking his suave business tone.

"Rollie. How are things?"

"Better than yours, I'll bet. Too busy even to check your caller ID?"

"I'm waiting for a call from Falkner while trying to juggle Jefferson."

"He, he. You're welcome," I laughed.

Chaos hated dealing with Falkner and had been trying to palm him off to me before my reassignment. He'd almost made it, too.

"Fuck you," was Chaos' response.

"Why doesn't Tank have him?"

"Jefferson?"

"Yup. I thought he was taking a bunch of my clients while I was gone?"

"He was. Is. Jefferson's complaining he's too intimidating. He wants to know when you'll be back."

"We've got…" I counted the days up in my head. "Two weeks of the tour left before they head back to the States." I sat up suddenly.

"I do know your schedule," he muttered.

But I wasn't listening. "I'm not going international, am I?"

"You don't get an Austin Powers moment, no."

"I was thinking Bond."

"Doesn't make it true."

"So, I suppose you think you're Bond?"

"What I am is a single guy with a beautiful woman waiting for him at home and too much work to do."

"Oh, please," I snorted. "Bert's fallen asleep on

her laptop again."

I could hear the smile in Chaos' voice. "Yeah, she probably has."

Bert was doing her PhD and every spare moment she had she was working on it. I mean, I went into the military to avoid proper university. Why Bert had voluntarily signed up for at least eight was beyond me. And that was only if she finished her dissertation by the end of the four-year guideline.

Chaos sighed heavily. "I think it's time, mate."

"What? You're retiring?"

Chaos barked a rough laugh. "No. I meant expanding."

"Look," I said. "I know we talked about us going interstate, but I'm happy in Adelaide. We've made a home. And we're not *quite* run off our feet."

"Firstly, we are totally run off our feet. Secondly,

I was floating the idea of hiring new blood, not sending you lot off to new lands in search of more gold."

"New blood?" I asked, perking up. "Like…add to the team?"

"I know it's a novel idea," Chaos laughed. "But it would help spread the load a little. Especially when we keep having these bigger jobs that pull us away from our usual routine. First Nico, then Tank and you…"

"You think we'll get more jobs like this?" I asked him.

"Not unless we get some new blood in. We just won't have time or opportunities."

"Who's gonna train them?"

"Well, it's not going to be you. Last thing I need is two of you."

I laughed. "The world could do with more me."

"No. It couldn't. I suppose it would have to be Tank. But I've got to talk to Hawk about it anyway."

"Well, for what it's worth, I think it's a…decent idea."

"Is that your unusually polite way of saying it's shit?"

"I didn't say that," I said with a smile.

"Not specifically, no."

"Nah, man. Go for it."

"You just want to piss Tank off with a new trainee."

Damn Chaos, knowing me so well.

"Maybe. It'd be fun to see if he had a threshold. Please say we can do a scholarship program and get proper greenies in?"

"We're definitely not doing that. Nico would

blow us all up for sure long before we found out if Tank had a threshold."

"But we could have a whole class. The Grace Grayson Academy. Training up elite security guards from all over the nation!"

"Let's see how one new recruit goes before we go all Police Academy on this, yeah?"

I snorted. "Sure, bossman."

The conversation lulled for a moment, me picturing the glory and prestige of Grace Grayson Academy and Chaos probably thinking about the six thousand ways it could go wrong.

"I'm guessing there's not much of anything to report, by the way?" he said.

"Not really. There was an incident on our first night here. A picture in her dressing room that Zach totally assures me could have been a *Firebird* reference. Other than that, it's still all online. I'm guessing Nico's keeping you updated on all of that?"

"He's monitoring and coordinating with Miss Fern about legitimacy of what he finds. We'll pass on anything that we deem an immediate threat."

I nodded, even if he couldn't see me. "Cool. Okay. Well keep me posted and don't miss me too much."

"I wouldn't dream of it."

I grinned, blew him a kiss and hung up.

I might have made a tit of myself in front of Nora, but I'd always have my team to go home to. I couldn't very well risk them living boring lives now, could I?

11
Nora

I'd seen a little bit inside the mask and I'd be lying if I said I didn't want more.

I'd thought his cheeky green eyes and cocky smirk were intriguing enough before? Now I'd glimpsed a little taste of the man behind them, I was even more interested in discovering his every little trait, his every thought, his whole life. I wanted to get to know him.

We were all in the green room on our third to last

stop of the whole tour. Five more concerts and we were done. We headed home. That was it.

Nate and Ryder were laughing about something over in the corner and I couldn't help but like the way Ryder seemed to fit in with the band so well. Even Brax, who took to absolutely nobody in the twenty or more years I'd known him, had been seen to crack a smile in the presence of Ryder Andrews' hilarity. The band liked him.

Nate had even stopped teasing about me liking him and I was sure that had more to do with how Nate felt about Ryder than it was a commentary on how he felt about me. I didn't know exactly what they'd bonded over – aside from their similar senses of humour – but it was obviously quite strong. Nate hadn't even had time to have a stupid argument with Brax for at least a week.

Ryder looked over to me – as always, checking where I was and making sure I was safe and secure – and smiled.

I felt my answering smile blossom involuntarily. Not that I wouldn't have smiled back, it was just quicker happening than I expected. It was an instant knee-jerk reaction I didn't even think about.

Worse was the fact I didn't just smile back at him, but I also dropped my eyes as I looked at him like I was playing coy. Also not a conscious action! Here I was, bassist to a world famous rockband and I was flirting with my security guard like we were on the middle school playground.

I told myself to ignore him and pretend he wasn't there. That was always my go-to for crushes on the playground. Of course, crushes on the playground had never liked me back and I had certainly never already slept with them.

I did a reasonable job of ignoring him until he crouched down next to my chair.

"You okay?" he asked.

"Fine."

"Can I get you anything?"

"No."

"Are you ignoring me?"

"Trying."

He cracked a laugh. "Why?"

I put down my tablet and looked at him. "I'm reading a very important book."

"Really? What is it?"

I looked around the room, but the only people in it were Zach, who was asleep with a book on his face, and Nate, who had his headphones on and was practicing with his drum pad.

"It's 'How to avoid shagging your security'," I told him.

"Oh, so you're in such danger of letting it happen – again – that you need professional advice?" he chuckled.

"Well, I wouldn't call it professional," I said, faux-dubiously. "I think she might give in."

"Oh, really?" he asked, interest firmly piqued.

"Really. But you know. She really shouldn't."

"Has she considered just how very good it was?" he asked.

"She has, but is that really a good reason to sleep with someone?"

Ryder scrubbed a hand over his chin. "Are you just turning all my preconceived notions on their head? Not sleeping with someone when it's amazingly good? Novel idea."

I smirked despite the mock-serious stance I was attempting to take. "This is serious business, Ryder. What's she supposed to do?"

"Well, I, personally, am all for the pursuit of pleasure."

"Even if it leads to things it shouldn't lead to?" I asked.

He hauled himself to standing with a grunt.

"I'm impressed you lasted down there as long as you did," I told him.

He winked. "It's all in the thighs." Then he got back to the task at hand. "Now, I would say – and this is new for me – I would say that wherever pleasure led maybe…just maybe it was supposed to lead there."

"That's a very philosophical view."

He shrugged and smiled. "I'm trying this new

thing."

"Oh, yeah?" I asked. "What sort of thing?"

"The kind where I let go a little."

"Is that a message?" I asked, my eyebrow rising in question.

He smirked. "Not at all. You want to let go? You let go. You don't? Well, you don't have to."

I got what he was saying. On both levels.

On the first, very simple level, he was saying that we made our own choices about our actions and no one else could make them for us.

On the second, and also quite simple, level, he was saying that whether we slept together again was up to me. He was up for it, but no worries if I wasn't.

"What do you do when you're not on tour with rockstars?" I asked him.

He looked genuinely surprised by that question.

"Uh," he chuckled. "I mostly stand around looking intimidating for men who wouldn't scare a church mouse if they didn't spend so much money pretending they could."

"So, you do security for a bunch of dodgy blokes?"

His eyes were alight with humour. "Dodgy is relative. Nothing illegal. That's not the Grace Grayson style."

"What is the Grace Grayson style?"

"If you ask the boss, it's finesse, loyalty, focus and professionalism."

"But I asked you."

"Then I'd say finesse, loyalty, focus and professionalism." He couldn't even finish the sentence without laughing. "No. Definitely loyalty. Lotta focus. We're professionals. But all that finesse stuff isn't me."

"What is you, then?"

He sighed. "That's a bloody good question. And you've had a lot of them," he said with a wry grin. "Do I get to ask any?"

I shrugged. "I don't see why not?"

"Who is Nora Curry really?"

"Woah, not pulling any punches, I see."

"Ask Tank. I don't pull punches."

"Who is Nora Curry?" I pondered, wondering what I'd tell him. "She's just a girl who learnt how to play bass guitar so she could hang out with her brother."

It wasn't a lie, but neither was it the full truth.

I'd learnt as a child that the world didn't care for who I was. So, I decided, if I couldn't be myself, I'd be outrageous and free to do what I wanted when I wanted. Only, it hadn't really been what I wanted. It had been what people wanted me to want; money, fame, guys.

Money was nice. It let me pay the bills and buy whatever book or clothes I wanted.

But I didn't need the fame. I could have easily lived without the fame. I would have happily lived without the fame…if I wasn't so used to the familiarity of it.

And guys? One guy was enough for me. Or would be, if I met the right one. My life had never really let me meet anyone who might have been close to the right one.

"A girl with a guitar," he mused. "Isn't that how all the best romances start?"

"What kind of romances are you reading?" I asked him with a humoured laugh.

As he walked away, he shrugged coyly. "Maybe I'm reading the wrong ones."

And maybe he wasn't.

Maybe my life had finally let me meet the right one and maybe I did want to see where things could go with him. But every time I tried to accept it and agree with his cocky teasing, I couldn't get the words out. One-Night Nora had become my shield against the world and I was too afraid of the consequences to lower it now.

12
Ryder

This whole thing was playing out like it had been carefully orchestrated by fate.

It was a wanky thing to think, but it felt true nevertheless.

How else did you explain two serial one-night stand artists coming together…or not as the case may be. All the signals had been there from the start. The attraction had been immediate and it had been epic. And yet? We didn't do anything about it right away.

Okay, I was taking too much credit.

She didn't do anything about it right away.

I'd been glad about that. I remembered thinking it the night we went clubbing, how different things might be had we slept together right off the bat. What I hadn't anticipated was just how much I wanted from her now I'd really gotten to know her. Except I hadn't really gotten to know her. I felt like I knew her. Who she was. The kind of person she was. I just didn't know all her hopes and dreams. I didn't know her favourite colour. I didn't know her favourite song.

I just knew that I could spend a lifetime getting to know every single detail about her and it wouldn't be enough. I also knew that none of those things were really important. Not as important as chemistry and laughter and really great sex. I knew I could spend an entire lifetime not knowing those things about her and I'd still want to be with her.

The problem I was facing was that maybe she didn't want to be with me.

She was attracted to me, all right. I saw it in the little glances. I saw it when I caught her looking at me when she thought I wouldn't notice while I was looking at her when I thought she wouldn't notice. That was different to when I was looking at her when she was allowed to notice because that was my job.

"Let me speak to Nico," I said to the room at large when I got the team on speakerphone.

"He doesn't want to speak to you," Hawk said.

"What?" I spluttered. "But I am His Awesomeness, Brilliance Extraordinaire. Baron of Brains. Count of Confidence. Duke of–"

"Dim-wittedness," I heard Nico's voice.

"Nico!" I cried happily. Anything that would annoy the *wittle* nerd.

"What do you want?" he sighed. "I've got nothing more for you. It's all the same. 'She loves me. We're destined. She'll know me.' Some *super* obscure and quite frankly far-reaching reference to birds and fire. I'm good, but I'm not magic."

"That's great and all," I told him. "Read your report. Thank you. Keep 'em coming. Bit of light reading before bed, really helps my nightmares come through. No, I need different help."

"I'm not giving you access to Nora's phone."

"You could do that?"

"I don't know. It was the most absurd thing I could think of. Maybe. Let's say yes. I'm still not doing it."

I nodded. "No. Fair. No, I want to know how you dealt with your raging attraction to your nerd queen while on mission."

"I think," Hawk interjected. "You'll find he *didn't*."

"Did Leah tell you that?" Nico huffed.

"I can't confirm or deny that Raegan has told the girls everything about your little lockdown," Hawk said calmly.

Oh, I so wished I was there to see Nico's little nerd head explode.

"For someone who spends his life uncovering people's dirty laundry, you sure hate sharing," I noted.

"I'm leaving now," Nico said.

"No!" I called. "I'm sorry. I legitimately need to know."

For something that had been initially intended as a joke at our resident nerd's expense, I now legitimately wanted his opinion.

"Rollie, just once can you keep it in your pants?" Chaos asked.

"My pants are not the issue here. Hers are. So, if you lot could kindly relate to me how you deal with not going mad over a girl, then I would be greatly appreciative."

"Again…" Hawk said. "I think you'll find we didn't. Why? You lusting after your rockstar, mate?" He sniggered.

"Say I was–"

"You're Rollie, you show her a brilliant time and everyone moves on with their lives," Hawk said. "I don't see the problem."

"Again with the…" Chaos muttered. "Can we not

have a single meeting where girl problems do not interfere with the business at hand?"

"No," Nico said.

"You may as well add it to the weekly agenda," I said.

"I'll do that!" I heard Flo in the background.

"Hey, Flo!" I called.

"Hello, Rollie," she called back and I heard the smile in her voice.

"I'm glad someone misses me," I said.

"Did you have anything to add to this meeting or were you just feeling lonely?" Hawk asked.

"I had very important other business," I said indignantly.

"Rollie, wanting to sleep with your charge is hardly important other business," Chaos said.

"It would be if it interfered with my ability to

secure her personal safety," I said carefully.

"Does it?"

I sighed. "No. I just need to know what to do. I'm losing my mind."

"Be careful with it," Nico drawled. "We'll need a microscope to find it again."

"Har-di-har," I said sarcastically. "If you won't help a brother in need, I'm going to take my ball and go home."

"Just be yourself," Nico offered. "That should put her right off and make the job easier."

I had to give him that one. It had to be said. It had to. It was too good an opportunity to miss.

"When you coming home, mate?" Hawk asked. "I think someone's gunning for office clown."

"Yes," Nico said, deadpan. "My ultimate goal in life. My secret, nefarious plans. How did you guess?"

"If it's really that big a problem for you," Chaos said to me, "my only suggestion for you is as many cold showers as it takes and a hefty dose of man the fuck up and control yourself."

"Well, who pissed in his coffee this morning?" I asked, then took the words in the manner in which they were intended. "You're right. I know. Man up and control myself. I can do that, surely."

"Unless…it's all because he *likes* her," Hawk teased.

I snorted. "Hey, just because you bozos let love smack you in the face and still didn't recognise it, doesn't mean we all will."

"Hang on. You love her?"

I had definitely not intended the discussion to go down this route and now I was stuck without a witty paddle with which to navigate the river of shit I found myself in.

"No," I answered. "But I'm open to the possibility with a woman I'm attracted to and I'm not afraid to fan some flames and see what's there."

"You do recall she's going back to the States after this tour?" Hawk said kindly. "She was only in the country this long because they had a deal to record here."

I nodded to myself. "And that means I should close myself to all possibility?"

"Maybe not in general," came Tank's rumble.

"Nice of you to join the party," I commented dryly.

"Just maybe with her," Chaos said.

It was easier said than done. I liked Nora. My newness at being open to love and being loved meant

I was excited about it. I wanted to find it. Maybe I was deluding myself into thinking it was possible with her. But less likely couples had found their happily ever afters.

Not that I said any of that to the team. It was better to let them think that happy-go-lucky Rollie was moving on with his life. Besides, if we could all put this little conversation behind us as an unintended interlude, that would be great.

"Yeah, you're right. Good point. I'm rushing into things."

"Okay. So, you're good?"

"Oh, I'm still mad attracted to her and will need a cold shower at the end of every day, but no one's professing their love to anyone," I told them, which at least wasn't a lie. "Is that all you need me for?"

"For interrupting our meeting and side-tracking

us from the agenda?" Chaos clarified.

I grinned. "Yeah, that."

"Yeah, man. That's all we needed you for."

"Cool. I'll check in tomorrow. Rollie, out!"

I hung up and flopped back on my bed.

I knew I was messed up about Nora. No version of Rollie went to the team for advice about girls without it being serious. But their advice had been sound; control yourself.

Control myself, it was such an easy solution. It was, after all, all about me and my actions. Nothing needed to be done about my crush or attraction – or whatever it was – to Nora. Literally. Nothing. I'd deal with it because it wasn't her problem.

I left my room and knocked on her door.

She opened it with a smile and stepped back to let me in.

"You could use the door card," she said.

"What if you weren't decent?" I replied.

"It's nothing you haven't seen before."

I tried my darndest not to look her over and remember exactly what she looked like, what she felt like, what she tasted like. I was dealing with it and controlling myself.

"Miss Fern wants us all in the conference room in ten minutes," I said.

Nora paused for a moment, clearly surprised by response or lack of. "Oh. Okay. No. Sure. Can do."

I gave her a nod. "I'll be outside."

She gave me a nod. "Okay, then."

See, I could totally do this control myself thing. Hawk better watch himself, because Rollie was actually not too bad at this fancy finesse stuff.

13
Nora

Something had happened and he was trying to hide his attraction to me all of a sudden. If it wasn't one of the most adorable things I'd ever seen… Well, however those phrases end, it was.

It was also one of the weirdest things I'd ever seen and I didn't like the way it made me feel.

I didn't know what had done it, but it felt like something needed to be put right between us.

"Ryder, can I ask you something?" I asked as I

threw my bag onto the hotel bed of our second to last tour stop.

"You can ask me anything you like," he answered.

I turned to look at him. "Did I…do something to annoy your or upset you or anything?"

He frowned. "No. Why?"

I shrugged. "You just seem different…the last day or so."

"I do? How?"

"I don't know."

Did I openly just say it was that he didn't flirt with me anymore, or wink at me, or even give me that crooked half-smile that made my insides all wibbly? I mean, he'd been doing it since the moment we'd met and now… The lack of it was deafening.

"Something seems…off?" I suggested.

By the look on his face, he knew something was off, too. I'd have said he knew exactly what was off, what I referring to, and that those two things were one and the same.

"Since we met, we've…" I paused, trying to search for the right word. "We've had a dynamic."

He nodded slowly. "Okay…?"

"I feel like maybe something happened to it, and I just… I thought we had a…chemistry?"

He seemed to pause, then a slow smile spread across his face.

"Exactly. Like there was something there," he said excitedly. "Something between us."

Again, I felt that hesitation to agree. Hesitation to admit that I thought there was definitely something between us. It was on the tip of my tongue, but I just couldn't do it.

"A physical attraction." I nodded.

Ryder opened his mouth like he was going to disagree, then seemed to change his mind. "A physical attraction," he agreed. "There's definitely been plenty of that."

"Good," I said. "I mean, I just wanted to check I wasn't making it all up in my head."

He looked at me like he was weighing something up in his mind. Finally, he opened his mouth.

"Nora, it's no surprise or secret that I've been into you since I met you. You're sexy, you're funny, you're smart. You know how to handle yourself. It's hot."

"Then why have you been so…weird the last couple of days?" I asked.

"Because I thought One-Night Nora was over it and acting like I had a second chance might have looked a little desperate," he said.

If there was a time to regret the nickname the tabloids had given me, it was now. Oh, I'd earned it. Fair and square. I wasn't complaining about that. I just noticed the lack of catchy alliteration being added to Coop or Zach or Brax or Nate, and they'd definitely earned themselves a moniker.

"I wasn't– I'm not over it," I told him. "I kept trying to tell myself I was, but then I just have to look at you – to think about you – and I want you all over again." I smiled at him, knowing I sounded corny enough to my own ears.

He didn't seem to think so though. "I'm glad," he said as he stepped towards me.

"You are?"

He nodded. "Because I've been thinking about kissing you every moment since I last did."

I bit my lip against a ridiculous smile that was threatening. "Is that so?"

"It is."

"Then, why don't you?"

"Is it what you want?"

"Yes," I told him, definitively. "Yes. I want you to kiss me."

He wasted no more time. His lips were on mine, claiming me as his in that moment. I kissed him back with all the hungry need I'd felt for him the past week.

Torn between thinking he was just doing a shy act and thinking he'd got over me had been a rollercoaster ride I never wanted to repeat. So, it didn't have to just be one night. I could admit that to myself – even to him if he asked – and not be promising anyone a future.

We made short work of each other's clothes and fell onto the bed with a shared laugh. His eyes shone. The humour in them infectious. I couldn't have wiped the smile off my face had I wanted to.

Ryder pulled me close and kissed me everywhere. His lips blazed a path across my skin like he was marking me as his. In the heat of the moment, I wasn't so opposed to the idea.

He ran his fingers between my legs. There was no teasing this time, there was only his fingers and my clit as he once again read my body's needs and desires plain as anything. It was all I could do to just hold on tight and let him work me to orgasm.

I was impatient to have him inside me, but he refused to move his hand, grinning all the time, until my body stopped twitching pleasantly at his touch and my breath returned to normal. It was only then that he let me go, with a kiss to the shoulder, to reach for a condom.

He let me roll it on him again and I revelled in the feeling of power it gave me. The way his eyes hooded as I ran my hands over him, the smile of satisfaction on his face. He looked at me not only as a woman who was pleasuring him, but as something that amazed him in its own right. Like I amazed him in my own right.

I pulled him on top of me this time, wanting to have him close, to put my arms around him, to feel his power as we came together.

As he thrust deep into me, my hands and eyes skimmed his body. His arms. His chest. His back. He was hard and muscular from years of training, I knew that now. The whole package was impressive. Not just his body, but who he was.

Once hadn't been enough.

I doubted twice would be either.

14
Ryder

The next night, after the concert, we were lying in bed again.

"Pfft," I scoffed. "I'll bet you were right popular at school."

Her scoff was far more disbelieving. "Um, no. Certainly not in middle school."

"What happened in middle school?" I asked her.

She shrugged and wouldn't meet my eye. I didn't feel inclined to encourage her to.

Finally, she said, "No one liked me."

I found that very hard to believe. "What?"

She nodded, sparing me a glance. "No. It's true. I was me, Nerdy Nora, and…well, they didn't dislike me, but no one…liked me."

"You mean guys hadn't yet caught on that nerdy girls are awesome?" I laughed.

She smiled, but shook her head. "No. I mean everyone. I had no friends. I didn't get invited anywhere. Not to parties or for sleepovers or even to sit with anyone at lunch. The only people who chose to talk to me were Cooper and his mates."

"So, it wasn't everyone?"

"They only bothered to talk to me because I could play bass and the only other option for a bass player was Icky Ricky in the year below them."

"Icky Ricky's a pretty catchy nickname."

Nora grimaced. "He was proper gross. Just kinda…slimy with the girls."

"Well, you've got no problems getting people to like you now."

"No."

Why did it sound like that was a bad thing?

"I realised when I was fifteen that I could just act differently, be different, and people would like me. A couple of girls at school saw Brax pick me up once and thought I had some hot older boyfriend. So, I pretended to care about clothes and makeup and boys, and I got invitations. Some days, I feel like I've completely lost myself and I'm drowning in this stranger."

I realised then that there were lots of ways you could lose yourself along the way. For me, it had been war. War had the ability to leave scars no one could see but that burrowed into your soul and bled a little out of you each day. For Nora, it had been loneliness. She had her own scars, and they'd bled badly in their own way.

I wasn't sure what to say to her. I wasn't the guy people came to when they needed to get real. I was the comic relief. I was the guy who prevented shit from getting too real in the first place. But I didn't want to do that with her. I wasn't uncomfortable with her real. I just didn't know what to say. So, I said nothing. Which, turned out, was probably worse than if I had let off a typical Rollie joke.

"Yeah, I get it," she said with a heavy sigh. "No baggage."

She made to get up and I stopped her.

"I'm fine with baggage," I said told her, meaning every word when it came to her. "I'm just not good at knowing what to say."

I could tell she thought I was just covering so I had a hope of getting her back in bed.

"You asked me what was me?" I said and she nodded. "I'm the guy who goes down the local gym on a Friday night and gets into the ring with some legitimate madmen all so I can outrun a past that might kill me if it catches me."

"Ryder…" she breathed.

"Look," I started, wondering where I was going with this. "You know how the Grace Grayson boys are all ex-military?"

She relaxed back onto the bed and nodded. "Yeah," she said slowly.

I nodded. "Right. Well, take military and add special ops to that."

"Really?"

I nodded. "It's not as glamorous as the books make it sound. We saw some shit. And, when I say shit…" I breathed out. "I mean some shit. It totally messed me up. It messed all of us up. But…" I hadn't realised I was going to get quite so real, but I was there now. "I handle it the worst out of all of us. You feel like you're drowning in a stranger?" I asked and she nodded. "I get that. I mean, the drowning part. I've always been the awkward kid who makes jokes to cover his insecurities."

"I have the music. I have the concerts. Each one is a checkpoint and, if I can make it to the next one, I can make it," she said.

I nodded. "I have my humour. I fight. I don't so much as deal with my shit as wallow in it for a while in safe doses."

"Oh," she sighed as she fell back against the bed.

"What I wouldn't give to just snuggle up at home in my oldest trackies with a tub of Rainbow Paddle Pop–"

"A tub?" I interrupted.

She smiled. "It comes in tubs – with a bottle or two of wine and some trashy rom-coms."

"If you've got coffee Giant Twins, I'll join you."

She nudged me. "Judge me all you want, I can take it."

I pulled her close. "No. Not at all. That does sound good."

"Even the trashy rom-coms?"

"*Die Hard*'s a romance."

"No," she laughed. "*Die Hard*'s a Christmas movie."

I think I might have fallen in love with her on the spot. "All right, we'll keep that one for Christmas

Eve."

"Oh, we will, will we?" she asked with a smile.

I shrugged. "Christmas isn't that far off."

She nodded. "No… It's not."

She was getting cagey again. The same way she did anytime mention of a time outside that moment came up. The Rollie of a couple of years ago was impressed by her determination to avoid anything but the here and now. The newer Rollie had to wonder if, like me, she'd be better off at the very least learning to consider the future rather than refuse to acknowledge its existence. Or maybe she was fine the way she was.

I definitely hadn't come to grips with actually considering the future in all my actions. I didn't stop to think about the future if there was a chance it could be unfavourable; I just acted. But I was trying to.

One thing I did know, though, was that it wouldn't do to push her if she wasn't ready. I could only keep doing what I was doing and hope my natural charm eventually won her over for good.

15
Nora

At the end of the concert that night, feeling giddy as anything, I skipped over to Ryder, beaming.

"We did it! We're almost home," I said as I launched myself into his arms.

He laughed. "You are. One more concert and that's the tour done."

I sighed as I leant my head against his chest, feeling a sense of contentment I didn't recall feeling in a long time, or possibly forever. Having him close was uplifting. It made me feel like I could do anything. Be anyone.

I didn't want to think about anything outside this bubble of time. Not about the future. Not about the past. Not about what other people would think about any of it. We were just two people peacefully coexisting together in a moment of perfection.

I reached up and pressed a quick kiss to his lips.

"Give him another one for us, love!" someone called.

Ryder and I turned.

It seemed our quiet little corner had been under surveillance. Two photo journalists had cameras pointed in our direction waiting for her to kiss me again.

I pulled away from Ryder just as Anton stalked over.

"You vultures know you're meant to wait in the green room," he said as he started dragging them away.

I didn't just pull away from Ryder, I stepped away. A good foot away. As far as it was possible to go without looking like I was moving and still get as far away as possible.

"Nora?" I heard Ryder ask.

But my eyes were focussed on the photographers Anton was leading away. How much had they caught? What were their editors going to say about it? What had one little moment of carelessness done?

****

By the next morning, it was all over the news.

'One-Night Nora no more: star in relationship

with her new bodyguard'

'One-Man Nora Curry's off the market'

'*Valjean* bassist Bodyguard, Ryder Andrews, last in long line of men?'

"Oh, they didn't even mention my name, but they mention his?" I huffed as I threw my tablet on the couch beside me.

I'd made it a point early on in my career not to go online as much as possible. I stayed clear of tabloids and avoided any platform that might have unfavourable news about the band. We had people who did that; waded through all the possible articles and only showed us the good stuff.

But I hadn't been able resist.

After getting caught with Ryder, I needed to know what they were saying. I needed to know how much damage had been done or if there was a chance to repair it.

So, I dived into the mess.

I went down the rabbit hole and got lost in the wormhole that was internet tabloids.

I didn't know how long I was there. I completely lost track of time. I only came out when I heard an insistent knock on the door.

"Nora? Nora, are you okay?" Nate was yelling.

I went and opened the door. As soon as he saw me, Nate grabbed my arms and looked me over like he was checking for outward signs of damage.

I pushed him off me and let him into my room. "What do you want?"

"I want to make sure you're okay," he said as I closed the door.

"Why wouldn't I be okay?" I asked, huffing a sarcastic laugh. "The whole world thinks I'm dating my security."

"Aren't you?"

I turned to him. "Excuse me?"

"Aren't you dating him?"

"No!" I said forcefully.

Nate held his hands up. "Okay. Calm the farm. You're not dating him. Could have fooled me, but whatever. With your coy smiles and eyelash flappery."

"Whatever for you, maybe," I muttered.

"Whatever for everyone."

"Says the man whose reputation isn't in the dirt."

Nate barked a laugh. "Your reputation is fine, Nora."

"Fine! Fine? Everyone thinks I'm dating Ryder!"

Nate nodded. "Yeah. And everyone is thrilled to bits for you."

I'd been waving my arms around hysterically, but I dropped them now and looked at him. "What?"

"Thrilled," he said, then added, "To bits. One-Night Nora's finally met her match and all that? News is abuzz with the excitement at what kind of guy could tame the wild girl of rock. They're saying it's the final step in Nora Curry's evolution from punk pin up to adult artist."

Where were all those articles in the rabbit hole? Where were those comments?

Actually, when I stopped to think about it, what I'd read had been masses of speculation, but no judgement.

"They…don't care?"

"Uh, the opposite actually. Everyone cares and think it's awesome. Brax threatened to kill him. Zach reminded him he's some black ops ninja. But Brax is totally ready to wail upon him at your behest. Even with the danger to his pretty face. And, look I'm more than happy to watch my brother get beaten up by a black ops ninja…"

"Ryder's not a black ops ninja and I don't want anyone to beat him up," I said, my brain moving too fast for me to keep up.

No one cared – as it were – if I was dating Ryder. My reputation was fine. Our music was fine.

I didn't know what I'd been so worked up about. This One-Night Nora reputation. Of course it wasn't everything.

Of course our true fans would be happy about something that made me happy. And if they didn't, screw them. We didn't need them.

Screw them. We didn't need them.

That was a new concept. One I hadn't considered.

I mean, we needed the fans. Without them, we couldn't feasibly keep doing what we loved to the extent we did it.

But we could have the power to write the narrative. We could actually do what we wanted – so long as it wasn't murdering puppies – and they'd be there with us for the ride. They wanted us to be happy.

Ryder would make me happy. I didn't know what the future could hold for us, but I wanted to see what we might have. I wanted to explore us, and more than in just the naked sense. As fun as that was.

I wished I'd realised that before I'd had the external validation. I wished I'd been strong enough to come to the conclusion without needing the people's approval. But I'd got there in the end.

Now, I had to work out how to tell him.

16
Ryder

"I'll leave you to get changed," I said to her, more curt than I intended.

Nora nodded. "Thanks."

I closed the door and stood outside it, reminding myself that this was why we didn't let our heart into things. This was *Valjean*'s last concert before heading back home to the States. And, as much as I held out hope that Nora might consider hanging around for a bit to see if there could be more between us, I didn't believe it for a second. She'd had chances. She'd had plenty of chances.

I just had to accept that, while I might have been worth more than a one-night stand, I wasn't worth that much more. Or, maybe I'd just been convenient. Who needs a one-night stand when you've got a bodyguard falling over himself to satisfy your every whim?

Those demons of mine had almost convinced me that it was the latter when I heard a shout from inside Nora's dressing room. Nora's shout.

I put a hand to the comms. "Trouble in Nora's room."

Barging into the room, I was on high alert. My senses were tuned and my adrenalin was spiking high.

Nora wasn't alone. There was a man in her

dressing room with her. A man I didn't recognise.

"Get out!" Nora shouted, holding a robe against her mostly naked body.

The man started singing, like some perverted version of a serenade. The tune was new to me, but I recognised the lyrics to *Firebird*. I could definitely understand why the sound of it scared Nora. It scared me. Sent goosebumps flaring to life across my body. Made me want to look over my shoulder in case the boogeyman was after me.

"Stop it!" Nora yelled and I could see she was on the verge of panicking.

I slid myself between Nora and the man, but it was like I was invisible to him. His eyes were firmly planted on Nora as he walked towards us. I backed Nora up slowly, trying to gauge the level of threat.

Clearly, my presence alone wasn't enough to

deter him or freak him out.

But how far was this going to go?

"All right," I told him, keeping Nora firmly behind me. "Time to go, mate."

I put a hand out to start pushing him out of the room, but he grabbed it.

Only then did he stop singing and look at me. He looked at me like I was nothing, just some minor inconvenience he needed to get rid of before he could claim his prize. Dude was like some freaky full-grown Annabel of some shit. That, coupled with the singing, put me right out. He was smaller than me and had zero fear or hesitation.

He took a swing at me and I ducked it.

"Ryder!" Nora called, worry evident in her tone.

That seemed to make the intruder even more pissed off with me. I was no longer an irrelevant annoyance. Whatever mission he was on, it was personal.

He ran at me with both hands bared. As my hands closed around his wrists and I struggled to keep him off me, Anton and Des ran into the room.

"Get her out of here!" I shouted.

They didn't ask questions. They did what they'd been trained to do; get the target out safely.

The intruder seemed to pause for a moment. Did he go after Nora or deal with me?

"Hey, dickweed," I said, throwing a punch to his face.

That decided him and I was (somewhat) glad when he picked me.

I was less so when it turned out his weedy, weedy stature hid a surprising amount of wallop. Wallop he wasn't scared of slamming straight into me.

He came at me, fists and nails flailing. Too many found their mark. The guy was just so erratic, I couldn't anticipate him.

Memories struggled for purchase on the surface of my mind and I shoved them away again. Now wasn't the time for reliving the past. Not when the future was at stake.

Finally, I got a couple of good swings in and took him down. It took all my body weight to keep him on the floor while I scrabbled for something to tie him up with. But the guy wriggled and squirmed, nearly bucking me off him.

"Stay. Down," I grunted, elbowing him in the back of the head.

His face hit the floor with an audible 'whack' and he was finally struggling less. I was able to tighten on of Nora's belts around his wrists and another on top of that just to make sure he wasn't going anywhere.

"Help me get him up," I said, seeing Anton in the doorway. "We got anywhere to put him?

Anton nodded. "We'll take him to the security office until the cops arrive."

Nora walked into the room as Anton helped me get the intruder up, visibly shaken, but standing tall.

"I thought you were getting her out of here?" I accused Anton.

"She's slippery," he said, giving her a side-eye.

"I had to know you were okay," she said.

"I had to borrow a couple of your belts," I told her.

She nodded. "Sure."

I paused on my way out. Nora's eyes flickered, full of concern, over my face and I doubted it was a pretty sight. I was sure I'd had worse, but not in a while.

"Are you okay?"

I nodded. "Fine. We'll get him out of your way."

She looked to the guy, who had deflated somewhat since I'd bound his hands. "Just so you know, I'm still performing tonight," she told him. "You've taken nothing from me."

His eyes lit up as she spoke to him, like he was under some delusion that she was speaking words of love and affection and giving him some promise that every word she sang was for him.

"Come on," I said, giving him a nudge, and Anton and I frog-marched him out of there to wait for the cops.

Nora took to the stage that night and reclaimed her song in a haunting acoustic version, accompanied by her brother on piano.

I caught the end of it after dealing with the police and watching the intruder being led away in proper cuffs. He was being charged with a bunch of stuff, including assault against me. I said I'd do what I could to help. Anything if it meant putting him away for as long as possible.

Nora's performance had taken my breath away and I knew then and there that, given half a chance, I'd fall totally, irrevocably in love with her. As it was, I didn't think I was getting out of this gig without some severe bruising on my heart as well as everywhere else.

After the concert ended, I ducked into Nora's dressing room. I could have slipped out of there without a backward glance. But that wasn't me. Not with her.

"I'm headed for the airport," I told her.

She frowned. "What? Right now?"

I nodded. "Job's done. Stalker's arrested. You're safe. Best I get out of your hair soon as poss."

She shook her head. "No."

"What do you mean, no?" I asked.

"I mean, no. You can't. Not yet. Not like this."

"Not like what? You don't need me anymore, Nora. You're safe. Anton and his guys have it from here."

She shook her head again. "No. No, you're wrong. I do need you."

If only it were true. "You'll be fine. You're headed home day after tomorrow anyway."

"I won't, Ryder."

"You will." I didn't know why she was so convinced. "He's gone away. He can't hurt you anymore."

"I'm not worried about him!" she cried.

"What are you worried about then?" I asked, totally confused.

"You!"

"What?"

"I... You. Us. I can't leave it like this."

"Like what? You want one more frolick in the hay before I leave?" I sounded frosty, but I didn't care.

"No. I want... I like you, Ryder."

"Well, good. Hate fuck's not really my style."

"No. I mean... I want to see if this could be something. No one cares." She threw her hands in the air and laughed like it was a good thing. "They don't care. It doesn't matter. I was worried about nothing. I denied how I felt about you for no reason. But I fell for you, Ryder. Totally, absolutely enamoured with you. So, I thought I might spend some time in Adelaide for a while and we can see where this goes?"

She was standing in front of me, saying all the things I wanted someone to say. Saying all the things I hadn't let myself believe I was worth for so many years. Saying all the things I wanted to hear *her* say.

But there was a bitter tinge to it. I couldn't lie.

I'd tried not paying attention to what the news was saying about us, what her fans' reaction was. I'd tried telling myself it didn't matter what other people thought about us. But it did. To her.

And I couldn't shake the feeling that she was only saying them now because the world had told her it was okay. The world was on board, so now she could get on board.

After everything I'd been through in my life, after

years of crippling inner pain, I finally believed I deserved better than that. I deserved to be wanted *despite* what other people said was okay, not *because*.

I shook my head. "I'm sorry, Nora," I told her, my voice catching slightly. "It does matter. I care." I shook my head again, everything in me screaming at me to shut up but I ploughed on anyway. "I care you couldn't see that before the rest of the world told you it was okay to be with me…"

I got where it came from; that need for external validation and the crippling fear of losing it and ending up with nothing and no one. I got it. But I didn't need external validation when it came to her. I didn't need to even tell my closest mates she existed before I knew I wanted to make a go of it with her. That's how sure I was about it.

I knew what anxiety did. I knew it fucked things up, made you make choices you regretted later. I knew how it could paralyse you. But I couldn't shake this feeling of betrayal. I couldn't see clearly beyond my own pain. I was blinded by this feeling that I was making progress with my self-growth and this just shat all over what I was finally believing about myself.

"I care I wasn't enough," I said softly. "I deserve to be enough."

Maybe it was self-love. Maybe it was selfish. Maybe it was time to put me first. Maybe it was the wrong time to put me first. Maybe my emotional range had hit tablespoon proportions. Maybe there was a piece of me that was using my new virtues as a crutch to continue old habits and keep me in my place.

But I wouldn't know what it was because I didn't stay to find out. I walked away. I walked away from the first woman I could see myself happy with, and I kicked myself the whole way.

17
Nora

I'd deserved that. I knew it. I'd been too weak to go for what I wanted without external approval and validation. I'd been so caught up in maintaining my image, being liked, that I'd chosen that over someone who could like me for all of me; old, new, famous, hidden.

A recent old me would have gone into defensive mode. I would have told myself that he wasn't worth it, wasn't worth my time. I would have turned it back on him. I would have repeated 'he doesn't matter' to myself until I believed it.

But he did matter.

He was worth it.

He was enough.

It might have hurt that he didn't trust my feelings for him when I expressed them to him. But I could also understand why he didn't trust them. I understood he had a duty to protect himself. It was about time he protected himself.

Just because he'd walked away didn't mean he felt nothing for me.

In fact, part of me hoped that, by needing to walk away, it showed just how much he did care and how much he'd have to lose if he trusted me.

Now all I had to do was show him I meant it.

Which was easier said than done.

I was back in the States and he was in sleepy little Adelaide.

With weeks of post-tour interviews coming up, I was starting to wonder if maybe it was a good thing we'd left things the way they were. We both had obligations on opposite sides of the world. I didn't expect him to drop his for me, and I couldn't just up and leave *Valjean*.

"For all that's fucking holy, shut up, Nate!" Brax huffed as they walked into the room.

"Hear me out," Nate said. "Coop's really good. We could 2Cellos this shit."

"No. You want to make a whole album based off classical music. Not the same."

"Nora?" Nate pleaded.

"Not getting involved guys," I told them.

"Tell him to at least consider it."

"I'm not fucking turning my guitar into a violin. It wouldn't even work."

"How do you know unless you try it?"

"I don't need to try it. They're two separate instruments."

"With that attitude they are."

"Still not going for it?" Coop asked as he wandered in.

"I've tried everything."

"You followed me to the loo, struck a jazz hands pose and said 'guitars, but wait for it, with bows…'," Brax said. "I thought you meant ribbons."

Nate pointed at him. "Could also work!"

"You are allowed a holiday," Cooper said. "Look at Zach."

We did.

Zach was asleep under his book and snoring

softly.

"I don't need a holiday. I need to work," Nate said, always itching to go, never able to sit still.

"You ever thought that maybe you use work as a distraction from an unsatisfactory personal life?" I asked him.

"Ouch," Nate said slowly. "Nora definitely needs a holiday."

"Nora needs a bottle of Jack and five minutes peace," I said as I stood up and walked out.

But maybe Nate was right. Maybe I did need a holiday.

The last tour would have been hectic enough without the stalker threat and without the added emotional complication of Ryder.

I felt like I was at breaking point. Something had to give if I wasn't going to completely implode. I already felt like I'd given up so much. I'd given up my freedom when *Valjean* had gone worldwide. I'd given up any kind of private life. I'd given up who I was – although that hadn't been entirely on purpose. And I'd not so much as given up as not given a chance to a guy who I could have had something very real with.

All for the sake of not putting other people out. All for the sake of being too scared to step into the uncertainty outside my comfort zone.

I was starting to get an inkling of how I could repair not only any chance of a relationship with Ryder, but also repair my relationship with myself.

Ryder had learnt to put himself first. Maybe at the worst possible time for me, but he'd done it. It was time I learnt to put myself first.

18
Ryder

"Hey," I said when she answered the phone.

"How are you?"

I nodded, not that she could see it. "Fine. You?"

"I'm…yeah. I'm good." A pause as she grumbled and chastised her brother in the background. "To what do I owe the pleasure?"

"You guys are probably super busy right now?"

I sounded whiny. I didn't do whiny.

"Well…" she said slowly. "Dinner is like…three

hours away and I'm supposed to be attempting a pavlova."

"All good."

"No. Why?" I think she'd cottoned onto my tone.

I sighed. "Nah, Bert," I told Hawk's little sister. "Bad timing. Dunno know why I called… All good, I'll see you at your parents' in a bit."

A door closed in the background. "Ryder Andrews," she said in her brook-no-argument voice. "What's the matter?"

"I…have an errand to run. I guess you could call it. I was kinda hoping for some…"

"Backup?" she suggested.

"Yeah. Why not."

"Okay…" She sounded like she was thinking so I didn't interrupt. "Text me where you want to meet me and give me… Uh… Pat does a better pav anyway... Give me fifteen minutes, plus travel time."

I smiled. "You sure?"

"Of course I'm sure. We'll head straight to Mum and Dad's from there. Okay?"

"Okay. Thanks, Bert."

"Brother of my brother," she said and I heard Chaos' words echoing in hers.

As I hung up, I wondered again why Hawk had been so against his little sister and his best friend hooking up. I got that there was the whole behind his back thing, but Kit Grayson and Amber Grace were so perfect for each other you'd be forgiven for thinking they were literally made for each other. It was as gross as it was inspiring.

Given I was far closer to our destination than Bert, I hung about the house aimlessly until it was time to leave, which I missed by ten minutes. I was still there before Bert, though.

Finally, Bert hurried up the street with a wave. "I know, I'm late. Kit thought I was being squirelly and I couldn't get out." She gave me a hug. "Okay, so *why* did you want to meet at…" She looked around. "A cat café?" I couldn't tell if she was amused or if she wasn't sure we were in the right place.

I shrugged nonchalantly. "I'm getting myself a Christmas present."

She looked at the café, then at me, back to the café, then back to me. "You're getting yourself a cat for Christmas?" she asked.

I nodded. "I'm getting myself a cat for Christmas."

"A cat? For Christmas?" she repeated.

"Yes. A cat. For Christmas. Problem?" I huffed.

"No." She shook her head and I could see she was hiding a smile. "No. Not at all."

"Seriously? What is so hilarious about me getting a cat?"

"Nothing until you got all weird about it."

I shrugged my shoulders. "I didn't get weird about it."

"You got weird about me getting weird about it."

"Okay. So, I think there's something weird about me getting a cat."

"Yeah, I'll say," Bert chuckled.

"So, you do think it's weird!" I accused her.

She shrugged as she made for the door. "Only because I thought you were a dog person."

That made me pause. "What exactly about me says dog person?" I asked her as I followed her inside.

She was already looking at the kittens. "I dunno. You just kinda scream dog person energy. Maybe it's 'cos you're so boisterous?"

"I haven't felt particularly boisterous lately," I said as we looked at the little balls of floof, incredibly sombre for me.

"No," she agreed. "I've noticed."

I sighed. "I've tried not to be."

Bert put her hand on my arm. "They understand. You should talk to them."

I nodded, knowing what she meant.

It seemed, one by one, the boys of Grace Grayson Security were having epiphany moments. And, one by one, these epiphany moments called for us to suck it up an get vulnerable with each other. I wasn't averse to vulnerability. It had a time and a place. But I preferred that time and place to not be in the near future.

We wandered around, had coffee, and played with the kittens while I tried to pick one.

"They're all super cute," I said to Bert.

"You can't take them all home."

"How many am I allowed before I become a crazy cat dude?"

"I think the established number is three."

"Three?" I asked and she nodded. "I guess I'll have to get them one at a time then."

There was one particular kitten who was trying to fight my shoelace. He – judging by the colour of his collar – was a fluffy tabby with hair sticking up at all angles. I picked him up and he mewed almost like it was a challenge.

"What about this guy?" I asked Bert, holding him out to her.

He licked her nose and she smiled. "I like him."

"I'm going to call him Arnold."

"Rimmer?" Bert asked.

I rolled my eyes. "Schwarzenegger."

"Duh," she said.

"Duh," I agreed.

Arnold wouldn't be ready to take home for another couple of days. It was a stupid rule, but suited me fine because then I could get everything ready for him. So, I paid for him and watched the café staff put a little sold marker on his collar, gave him one more hug, and Bert and I left arm-in-arm.

"How long until I see a kitten at the Grace-Grayson penthouse?" I joked.

"Uh, a while. I can barely look after myself, let alone a small being."

"Isn't that what Chaos is for?" I teased.

She nodded. "Uh, yes. Definitely. But I'd like him to have less responsibility, not more. And full time caring for my academic butt is a rather large responsibility."

"I'd thank you to keep your bedroom shenanigans to yourself."

She elbowed me playfully. "Funny."

I nodded. "I know."

We laughed and headed for her parents' place where everyone would soon be for the newly annual Grace-Grayson family Christmas do.

We walked in and Angus Grayson did a double-take.

"Toady!" I cried, my arms open.

I might have felt like utter and absolute crap, but it was my duty to make sure everyone had a good time.

"You're not my brother," he said, still looking between me and Bert like he was confused about something.

"No," Bert said, her mouth already full of whatever her Mum was working on in the kitchen. "I had to help Rollie with a top-secret mission."

"What gave it away?" I asked Angus. "Was it that I'm just too damn good looking to be your brother?" I gave him a wink.

"That is definitely it," Chaos said from behind me.

"That you, Rollie?" I heard Bert and Hawk's mum call from the kitchen.

"Hey, Mags!"

"Rollie, dear, can you grab the square platter off the table in the front dining room?" That was Chaos' mum Angela.

"Can do."

From there, it was hustle and bustle. Same as any dinner with the Grace Grayson clans. Phil and Rich made sure nothing on the BBQ or Webber got burnt. It was purely for show, while their wives were finishing things off inside. The kids tried to all hang in the backyard, but were put to use fetching and carrying for Angela and Mags whenever they were caught inside after another drink.

The whole atmosphere was of one big happy family, both blood and chosen.

Raegan was having her first Grace Grayson party, but she fit in like she'd been to every single one. Nico sat back in his usual corner chair and watched her bubble over excitedly.

Leah and Hawk were there, being as mushy as usual.

Chaos and Bert were even worse.

Angus, Tank and I were the only singletons left at the ball.

Seeing all the happy couples was a little painful, I wasn't going to lie. I knew for certain now that I wanted someone special of my own. I wholeheartedly believed I was worth it, that I could have it. I also, for a fleeting moment, thought I'd found that someone. But I'd done a typical Rollie and gone and fucked it up.

I should have known the boys would notice my mood and feel something had to be done about it.

"Come on," Hawk nudged me as he passed me a beer. "How you feeling? What's up? Who needs a beating?"

"How about me?" I asked, tipping the beer to my lips.

Chaos nodded thoughtfully as he took a sip. "Can be arranged. But is it what you really want?"

"You know what I want," I told him in a huff.

Another nod, this one from Hawk. "That I do." He clapped me on the back. "We've all been there, man."

I looked at Leah on the other side of his parents' backyard and gave a resigned sigh.

They had. Well, all except Tank. They'd all hit their low points where they thought it wasn't going to work out with their girls. We might not have known Chaos' for what it was when it happened. We might have thought Hawk was overreacting a little. We might have been in awe when it was Nico's turn.

"Well, now it's my turn, apparently," I grumbled.

"Talk to us, Rollie," Chaos said softly.

I shrugged. "What's there to talk about? At least

when you wankers fell for a girl, she lived in the same country as you. Nora and I could have had something. But we'll never know because I *'wanted more'* and walked away. Now she's back in the States and I'm here in sunny old, unchanging Adelaide."

"Have you tried talking to her?"

I looked at him. "How am I going to do that?" I mimed putting my phone to my ear. "'Yup. Nora, hey. Sorry. Look, my bad. I maybe shouldn't have thought I deserved something more and walked away. Shall one of us hop on a plane for a million years and we can talk this thing through?'"

"He still bitching?" Nico asked as he came up to us.

"I'll show you bitching. Right in the face," I warned him.

Nico hid a smirk behind his drink. "What? I thought maybe we'd moved onto the planning phase."

"What planning phase?" I huffed.

"You're the optimistic one, dude," Nico said. "If anyone can find a way to get a girl back, it's you."

"How many times do I have to remind you lot, she's on the other side of the world. It's probably snowing for Christmas. And what do we have? Buckets of sunshine and not even a whispy cloud in sight. I'm wearing nothing but fucking boardies and I'm still sweating. It's indecent."

"It's Christmas," Hawk laughed. "What else do you expect?"

"Leave him alone," came Tank's gentle rumble.

"Yeah, you can talk," I snapped. "You're the reason I'm in this mess."

"Ye-es," Hawk said sarcastically. "It's definitely Tank's fault you went and fell in love with a famous rockstar."

"I didn't..." I started, all ready for a fight. Then I sighed. "Well, I won't know what it could have been now, will I?"

"Now, who's got the emotional range of a teaspoon?" Nico teased, but I wasn't in the mood.

Tank put his hand on my shoulder and the affection I felt with all of them hit me right in the feels. I'd be nowhere without this group of arseholes. I'd be nothing. I'd be shrapnel on the side of some building long before now. More than that, I'd still be the emotionally stunted, insecure little guy who hid all his faults behind false bravado.

These guys had seen through the bullshit. They'd known the bullshit for what it was and still loved me anyway. They'd let me continue the façade because we all needed a laugh now and then, but they weren't afraid to be there for me when I needed it. Same way I wasn't afraid to be there for them when they needed it.

They were my brothers in all but blood and I didn't know what I'd do without them.

"I love you arseholes," I said with a rough chuckle, totally pretending I wasn't about to start tearing up.

"We love you too, man," Chaos said with a smile.

"Group hug!" Hawk cried and we all laughed as we became a jumble of limbs.

So, I might have lost the girl and lost all hope of getting her back, but I had my family. As far as consolation prizes went, they were pretty damn good.

19
Nora

I was beginning to hate interviews. I knew they were important to maintain post-tour hype. I knew they helped sales and streams. I knew they were good for the brand, and what was good for the brand was good for us and our music.

But, boy did they suck when you were stuck in your sixth one in two weeks in all that makeup under all those hot lights. Eight months on tour had given my skin enough problems I'd still be sorting them out when the next tour started. I didn't need to keep aggravating it now.

Still, one more. A last one. Just me this time with super daytime TV host Laine Campbell. Laine had been good to us over the years, by which I mean me. The boys were excellent eye candy for her viewers, but when it came to interviews they liked the female perspective. I'd been a guest quite a few times.

It was the perfect place and time to make my announcement.

I waited through the stack of usual and expected questions, then took my chance in a break.

"So, I guess now's as good as ever to announce I'm going to be taking a break from the band," I told her.

I could see her surprise as she surreptitiously looked at her notes to see if that topic was on them.

"You are?"

I nodded.

I'd talked to the boys about it, but no one else. Except Emma. Understandably, they'd been upset that we'd be apart for a while, but once I'd sat them down and explained how I was feeling they understood. Unanimously, they'd all agreed that if time off was what I needed then time off was what I had to have.

"I am."

"And what are you going to do on your…?"

"Shall we call it a sabbatical?" I said with a smile.

"Your sabbatical," she said.

I shrugged, cool and casual and calm. "I've been thinking about heading home to see my parents. Spend some well-earned time with them."

"And your brother?"

"He'll visit, I'm sure. Won't want to risk me becoming Mum and Dad's favourite."

She laughed. "Does this have anything to do with the bodyguard you were rumoured to be dating? He works for a company from your home town, doesn't he?"

I liked how Laine didn't name it. I wasn't surprised. If I ever mentioned Adelaide in the States, no one had any idea what side of the country it was on, let alone that it existed.

I nodded, acting cagey just like the fans liked. "It might. It might not," I laughed at my own joke. "No, really, it's about me. Getting back to my roots and finding a few things I've lost over the years. About finding myself again."

"Are you worried your music has suffered because of what you've been through over the last few months?"

I knew she was referring to the stalker and I wished I hadn't brought up taboo topics and given her the feeling she could bring up more taboo topics.

"I'll always worry my music suffers, no matter what does and doesn't happen in my life. I'll worry it's losing touch. I'll worry it's not relevant. I'll worry it's plain crap." It was the kind of waffling rock answer that we'd become master crafters of over the years. "Sometimes, we've got to sit back and take stock, you know?"

Laine nodded like she had any idea. "I do, yeah. So, back home. How long for?"

"I don't know yet. See where the mood takes me. How long it takes to find whatever missing piece I'm looking for. Maybe the boys'll do better without me and pay me to stay away."

"Maybe they'll do terribly and pay you to come back."

Oh, we laughed like that was hilarious. It was hilarious. It was a hilarious notion.

The boys would be fine without me. They might not remember where they left their pants or their phones, but they'd physically survive. And, they'd still have Emma.

They – by which I mean Nate – were already scheduling Skype dates and trying to remember the time differences. Brax was making sure I could still collaborate on songs if I wanted to or they needed me 'real quick' for something tricky. Zach was writing me a 'must read' list for all my down time and had decided we could have a book club to talk about it. And Coop was making sure Mum and Dad had the fastest internet Australia could provide – cue snort at that notion, because it wasn't very fast at all.

"They've promised not to replace me," I told her. "But I'm sure that just means they won't let all their famous collabs sign any permanent contracts."

"You're not worried it'll cause a rift? Worried the world will see the end of *Valjean* as we know it?" I almost applauded her on her dramatic voice.

"It's my brother and his three wanker mates from high school," I scoffed. "Nah, I'm not worried." My true-blue Aussie-ness was coming out now, as it inevitably did during interviews.

We'd agreed as a band early on that we'd try and sell our Australian-ness. We thought it could be a novelty we traded on. Like, this is the reason we're different from what you normally hear, because we're nuts. And the Luck of the Glenn-ish had held and it had worked for us. So, we used it to our advantage at every opportunity.

"What do your parents think about you coming home? They must be happy?"

I nodded. "I don't think they imagined their rockstar twenty-seven-year-old daughter would ever move back in with them, but..." I shrugged. "Shit happens."

"Well, I can certainly say I, for one, will miss you, and I'm sure I'm not the only one."

"Thanks, Laine.

"This has been Nora Curry, bassist from *Valjean*, who's just announced she's going on sabbatical. Tune in next for great winter warming ideas with Karen."

The show went to ads and I was released – mostly – from my stage persona.

"Thanks, Laine."

"You'll call me as soon as you're coming back, won't you?" she asked.

I nodded. "Sure."

I mean, I probably wouldn't. But it wasn't like I'd tell anyone else.

With that out of the way, I had a bunch of tearful arseholes to hug goodbye and a plane to catch.

20
Ryder

I was watching Arnold gambol about on the floor with the end of his feather toy instead of getting dressed for Nelson's end of year shindig.

We weren't even working; we were guests. I should have been excited, but all I could do was sit on the couch in my 'Nora ♡'s Ryder' t-shirt and stare at my kitten and wish I could be that happy and innocent again.

So, when my doorbell rang, I wasn't really

thinking about who it could be or what I was supposed to be doing. I walked to the front door in some kind of stupor and tried – and failed – to give myself a pep talk to get my sorry act together. After all, it was my fault I'd lost the girl. She was right there and I'd stupidly walked away. I was going to have to get over it at some point.

"Ryder…" said girl said as I pulled the door open.

I blinked. "Is this a dream?"

"Not a nightmare, I hope," she said with a forced chuckle.

I blinked again. "Uh… Aren't you on the other side of the world?"

She nodded. "Not so much…"

Well, obviously. She was standing right in front of me. "Right. No." I nodded.

"I was hoping we could talk?" she asked.

I looked around like I was wondering where to put her or something.

"Uh, sure. Come on in."

No questions about how she knew my address. No apologies about the state of the house. Just get right into it.

"I just… I had half a mind to do the whole boombox thing, but…" she trailed off. "We hadn't seen that one yet."

Guessing she meant movie, I shook my head. "One of many."

She nodded. "Yes. Look, about that… I've been thinking a lot about what you said. A lot. And, uh, well I'd like to think I've been doing some soul searching."

Arnold lolloped out from the living room and mewed at Nora.

"Oh, you've got…" she started.

"Arnold's new."

"Vosloo?" she asked.

I frowned. "What? Schwarzenegger."

She nodded. "Of course."

"Of course," I agreed.

We stood awkwardly for a moment and I realised it was the first time I'd really felt awkward around her. Like ever. Even just before I'd walked away, I hadn't felt awkward. It just made me feel like a prat. She'd come all this fucking way and I was standing around like a dick in a 'Nora ♡'s Ryder' custom *Valjean* shirt.

"Uh, sorry," I said. "I mean, more than the…" I motioned to the whole house, the situation, just all of it.

She gave me a small smile. "No. Not at all. I'm

sorry I just turned up unannounced."

I shook my head. "I'm sorry about…the way we – I – left things."

"There were a lot of things I should have done differently. A lot of things I should have told you, and earlier."

Now she was in front of me, I didn't think I cared. I simultaneously wanted to tell her to go back home and wanted her in my arms. I didn't think anything could change the conflict between what I wanted and what I expected would be the outcome of this; her going back home and me still wallowing. But then she continued.

"I'm the rock and you're the roll," she said. "And my rock is nothing without your roll." She seemed to catch herself and corrected, "My rock is an independent woman re-learning to trust her own self-worth, but she really, *really* likes your roll."

"I thought you were on a break from the band," was what my petulant inner-child popped out with.

Nora nodded. "Okay. I am. You can take the girl out of rock, but you'll never take rock out of the girl."

I couldn't deny she was winning me over. I'd missed her. I hadn't wanted to walk away in the first place, but I'd wanted more than just a relationship because the public approved of One-Night Nora finally having two – or more – nights.

But she'd left all that behind. She'd walked away from the one thing that had kept her anchored in the world. I admired her for that. And she'd walked – almost – straight to me. That had to count for something. Something that meant she wasn't just going to turn around and leave me without her.

"You're the rock and I'm the roll?" I asked.

She nodded, then stopped. "Your mates call you Rollie right?"

I smirked and nodded. "They do."

She sighed and a small smile broke through her uncertainty. "Thank God. I thought I'd come up with this awesome analogy and then totally cocked it up at the last minute."

I shook my head. "Nah. It works."

"It works? Or, *it works*?"

I couldn't help but laugh. "It *works*," I told her as I reached out to her and she took my hands. "It really works. I like it. I like you, Nora. But you know that."

She looked at our hands, a soft smile on her face. "I hoped you still did. But the important thing is if you can forgive me?"

I was about to blurt out that of course I forgave

her. As if I couldn't forgive her. But that was old, live nowhere-but-the-moment Rollie. New Rollie wasn't going to live anywhere-but-the-moment, but he was also going to take a second to consider the future.

"I want to forgive you, Nora–"

She nodded. "I get it."

I huffed a laugh. "Give me a second here. I'm not saying I can't."

Nora looked up. "Sorry. Assumptions. Continue."

I smiled. "I'm just…" Now I had the floor, I wasn't quite sure how to put it. "I'm a little unsure. But I don't want to be. I want to trust in you – in us – but I guess I just need you to know that I only need *your* permission for us. I don't care about what the rest of the world thinks, and you shouldn't either."

"I know. I'm working on it–"

"And I'm also sorry."

Now she frowned. "Sorry for what?"

"I'm sorry I just walked away. I should have just talked to you about it all then. I should have just been happy you wanted me and we could deal with the whole rest of the world's approval thing later."

She threw her arms around me and, God, did it feel good to have her in my arms again.

"I get it," she said. "I do wish you hadn't walked away, but I get why you did. It wasn't fair. I wasn't fair. I shouldn't have waited until it felt safe to admit I liked you. I should have been strong enough to just do it from the moment I met you."

"Oh, the moment you met me?" I teased.

She grinned and buried her face in my chest. "I'm sorry."

I held her tighter. "Can we agree we both

employed a shameful amount of arrogance and a ridiculous lack of communication, and put it all behind us?"

She nodded against me. "I definitely can."

"Good." We stood and just hugged for a while longer. Finally, I asked, "Exactly how long are you planning this break from the band?"

I felt her shrug. "Long enough to find myself."

I rolled my eyes. "Yeah, you said that in your interview."

She pulled away to look at me. "You watched my interview?"

"I read the bits that Flo shoved in my face."

I'd read maybe two lines that Flo had shoved in my face, had a hissy fit, and stormed off to my office telling them all that the next person who mentioned Nora or *Valjean* was cruising for a bruising. Those words. Exactly. I thought it best not to tell Nora just how cool I was.

Nora looked me over. "I don't know how long I'm taking off yet. Maybe I'll never go back. I didn't like who I'd become so I'm sure as hell not going back until I can make sure I'll never be her again."

I wanted nothing more than to take her to my bed and stay there all night, but I just remembered I had a party to get to.

"Uh…" I started. "Look. I really want to finish this whole…thing, but I'm actually supposed to be at a…thing."

"Oh," she suddenly looked super awkward. "Oh, sorry. I should have… We can pick this up later."

"No," I said quickly. "I mean, why don't you come with me?" I asked. "It's a client's big New Year's Eve thing. He's invited us as just guests this year and…well, he's a good mate and I can't really miss it. Even for…"

"Even for?" she asked.

I smiled. "Even for a girl I really, *really* like."

She smiled as well. "I could come. I've got my whole suitcase in the car. Plenty of choices of clothes."

I looked behind her and noticed the sleek black car parked at the curb.

"How long do you need?" I asked her.

"What do you need me in?"

"Got anything black tie ready to go?"

I followed her out to the car to get her suitcase. "Just what kind of high falluting friends do you have, Mr Andrews?"

"Just wait, you'll see."

We got ready with much checking each other out

and teasing about wasting time on horizonal – or vertical – shenanigans, and finally got to Ayer's House where Mr Nelson held his New Year's Eve party.

"Ryder Andrews, there you are!" Nelson called as we walked towards the door.

"I know," I told him as he hugged me. "I'm late. Sorry. But," I pointed to Nora, "I had an unexpected international visitor."

It took Nelson a few seconds to recognise her. Then his mouth dropped open. "Oh, my stars, Nora Curry! At my party." Nelson looked me up and down. "And with you." He gave me a wink. "Well done." Then turned to Nora. "Huge welcome, lovely to have you. Go in and make yourselves at home. I'll catch up with you later."

Raegan and Bert were the first two to spot us. I

couldn't tell if they were excited to meet the Nora Curry in person, or if it was because I'd got the girl.

"Oh my, God!" Bert said as she rushed towards us.

I thought she was going to launch herself on Nora, but she hugged me instead.

"See! I knew you could do it. What did you say?"

I laughed. "I didn't say much of anything. Nora came to me."

Bert sniffed. "Stop. Really? That's so sweet. Oh my, God. I don't know why I'm tearing up," she said with a laugh.

Raegan put her hand out. "Raegan Lane. Ryder helped me decode Nico."

Nora shook her hand. "And, Nico is the…tech guy?"

Raegan nodded.

While the three of them got to know each other, I looked at them and pictured Leah beside them. They were an eclectic bunch of girls, perfectly suited to an eclectic bunch of guys. As I was thinking this, Petra happened to come up and stand between Bert and Raegan and I decided she quite suited the group as well.

Then Leah and Hawk were there and I didn't have to imagine anymore.

Bert. Leah. Raegan. Nora. Petra.

It worked and I wasn't going to let anyone tell me otherwise.

Someone, though, maybe needed to tell Tank to lock that shit down before she moved on to less oblivious pastures.

"Bert, bubbles?" Hawk asked his little sister and I realised they'd all done introductions while I was working out how to get Petra and Tank together.

She shook her head. "No, thanks."

"You all right?" Petra asked.

"Yeah, fine. Ate too much, feeling a bit…ick." She rubbed her stomach.

Petra nodded. "I told you to lay off the profiteroles."

Bert smiled. "But they're so yummy, sitting there with their little soft deliciousness all begging to be eaten."

"Yeah," Petra huffed. "And now you've given yourself a tummy ache like you're five and can't control yourself at a party."

Bert looked at her seriously. "But I can't control myself at a party."

We all laughed at that.

"Right, I either need another drink or a dance,"

Petra said, looking around.

"I know what you're looking for." Bert nudged her.

"What am I looking for?" Petra asked, nonchalantly, still looking around.

"It starts with 'T' and ends with 'ank'," I said and Petra batted me playfully.

"I'm not doing anything."

"You know…" Hawk said slowly. "That's four down. There's only one to go."

I nodded thoughtfully. "That's right. And it does just so happen to be Tank."

Petra gave me a knowing look. "I don't know what you're talking about."

"They're talking about you finally womaning up and making Tank your man," Bert said helpfully, throwing me a shit-eating grin.

Petra's mouth dropped open like she'd been betrayed. "Who told you?"

"You," I laughed. "Every single time I see you."

Petra batted her eyelids. "Yes, all right. I suppose you've discovered my secret."

It was hardly a secret. Every time I went into Petra's shop for a fitting – it was the only place the Grace Grayson team even thought about buying our suits – she mentioned something about how she'd quite like to have her way with the gentle giant.

"Oi, Tank!" I called and he turned around.

He saw me waving and came over, giving polite smiles to Petra and Bert, and doing the standard introductions with Nora.

None of us knew what he wanted in a partner. None of us knew what he thought about Petra. But I'd be damned if the nicest one of us bastards went without love for a second longer than he had to. If any of us deserved it, Tank did.

"Petra needs a dance partner," Hawk told him.

Tank looked for a moment like he was about to ask what that had to do with him, but then the lightbulb went off and he just held his hand out to her and gave a short bow.

"May I have this dance?" he asked.

"We thought you'd never ask," Bert said, nudging Petra into Tank.

Petra, for all her assertiveness and strength and dirty mouth, looked out of her depth for a moment. It was quite possibly even uncertainty on her face. But, it was soon righted as Tank took her hand, laid it very gently on his arm, and walked her to the dance floor.

"Thank God," came a very recognisable voice and

I found Mrs Fortescue at my elbow.

"This your handiwork?" Hawk asked her?

"Mrs Fortescue's Matchmaking Services still going strong?" Leah added.

Mrs Fortescue touched the pearls at her neck and looked around the room innocently. "I don't know what you mean, dear. I just suggested that Miss Walsh would make a fine addition to his party and wasn't it a shame that young Gavin didn't have a date."

"Yeah, I'll bet," Nico muttered and he and Mrs Fortescue shared a smile.

"Now, I have yet to meet this ravishing creature, Ryder."

I introduced her to Nora, and we all spent a great deal catching her up on our activities until she was desperately needed somewhere else and she sashayed away in the glamourous way she'd arrived.

The time passed in a blur of friendship and camaraderie until the countdown to midnight was eventually approaching and people around the room were starting to find their loved ones.

As the cries of "Happy New Year" rang around us, I kissed Nora. That little happy bubble swelled in my chest and I didn't regret a single thing. Except maybe how stupid I'd been.

The road ahead was uncertain, but I was tired of running. I was tired of hiding. I deserved to let my future overshadow my past. I deserved to let go and live my life. My own life. Not just a life of making everyone around me laugh – although, I wasn't giving that up any time soon – but a life of my own where I could laugh as well.

Maybe Nora and I would make it. Maybe we

wouldn't. We weren't just exploring a new relationship but new – or, rather, old – selves. But we'd never know if we didn't try.

I wasn't worried though.

Rock and roll belonged together. It just made sense.

Grace Grayson Security

The Grace Grayson team all have their own story to tell.

Next up is Tank. Read on for more info.

Tank & the Rebel

See what all your favourite characters are up to down the track and maybe meet some new ones in Tank's story.

PETRA
I was the juvenile delinquent now in her late-twenties and with very little hope in sight. But I got along okay. I had a good group of friends, some delicious eye-candy, and my business was growing in leaps and bounds. Going out for a few benders with the girls of a Saturday night was what being in your twenties was all about. Right? Who needed to settle down?
My life is mess and disorder, but maybe there's one man who'll make me want to straighten it out.

GAVIN
When I was younger, they called me the gentle giant. I was actually one of the most picked on kids at school because I refused to return a punch. It wasn't just that I knew, as the biggest kid, I'd get into the biggest trouble. I just didn't like trouble. Odd then that I ended up in the Navy and turning a blind eye to the antics of the Grace Grayson boys.
My life is ordered and stable, but maybe there's one rebel who'll make me want to shake it up.

[Buy now.](#)

Rollie & the Rocker

Thank you so much for reading this story! Word of mouth is super valuable to authors. So, if you have a few moments to rate/review Nora and Ryder's story – or, even just pass it on to a friend – I would be really appreciative.

Have you looked for my books in store, or at your local or school library and can't find them? Just let your friendly staff member or librarian know that they can order copies directly from LightningSource/Ingram.

If you want to keep up to date with my new releases, rambles and writing progress, sign up to my newsletter at https://landing.mailerlite.com/webforms/landing/y1n6q2.

Follow me:

Thanks

I have never hated a book as much as I hated this one. Writing, that is. I could easily come up with a list of books I hated reading more than I hated reading this one, so that's something.

Six months, and still I had no plan for it. Still no ideas for scenes. Still nothing other than a few choice Rollie lines bumping around my head. It sucked. It was stressful. I am so glad it's over.

What sucks more is that I absolutely loved Rollie in the lead-up and I don't know why he was so uncooperative when it came to his own story. I guess that's just like him, though; make other people happy but not wanting to bother anyone with his own stuff.

I think what I ended up with is fine, but getting it out onto paper were possibly the worst four days of my life.

Still, I made it and it is in no small part due to my husband, my mum, and Charny, who are always by my side and in my corner cheering me on. So, thank you for believing in me when I forget to.

My Books

I'm working on my adult list, but you can find out about what I have planned at my website, as well as have a look at my older YA books;

www.elizabethstevens.com.au/after-dark.

About the Author

Writer. Reader. Perpetual student. Nerd.

Born in New Zealand to a Brit and an Australian, I am a writer with a passion for all things storytelling. I love reading, writing, TV and movies, gaming, and spending time with family and friends. I am an avid fan of British comedy, superheroes, and SuperWhoLock. I have too many favourite books, but I fell in love with reading after Isobelle Carmody's *Obernewtyn*. I am obsessed with all things mythological – my current focus being old-style Irish faeries. I live in Adelaide (South Australia) with my long-suffering husband, delirious dog, mad cat, two chickens, and a lazy turtle.

Contact me:
Email: contact@elizabethstevens.com.au
Website: www.elizabethstevens.com.au
Twitter: www.twitter.com/writer_iz
Instagram: www.instagram.com/writeriz
Facebook: https://www.facebook.com/elizabethstevens88/

Lightning Source UK Ltd.
Milton Keynes UK
UKHW010923021121
393249UK00001B/276